THESIS

BOOK 1 of INTERDISCIPLINARY

PAULINE UGALDE

BLUE FORGE PRESS
Port Orchard ✸ Washington

Thesis (Interdisciplinary, Book 1)
Copyright 2025
by Pauline Ugalde

First eBook Edition October 2025
First Print Edition October 2025

ISBN 979-8-89439-061-1

For information about film, reprint or other subsidiary rights, contact: blueforgegroup@gmail.com

Blue Forge Press is the print division of the volunteer-run, federal 501(c)3 nonprofit, Blue Legacy (EIN 83-4307421), founded in 1989 and dedicated to supporting artisans marginalized due to race, age, disability, economics or other factors. We strive to empower storytellers from all walks of life with our four divisions: Blue Forge Press, Blue Forge Films, Blue Forge Gaming, and Blue Forge Sound. Find out more at www.BlueForgeGroup.org

Blue Forge Press
7419 Ebbert Drive Southeast
Port Orchard, Washington 98367
blueforgepress@gmail.com
360-550-2071 ph.txt

To Eben Sherwood—

You affirmed and reaffirmed
that the future is ours to decide,
multiple times over.

THESIS

BOOK 1 of INTERDISCIPLINARY

PAULINE UGALDE

1

EDITING BAY, KESS BUILDING, RENEWED UNIVERSITY, I

Muta hurries around the bare editing bay again. Their eyes flick to the impatient mechanical keyboard, modified in haste before they ran out the door. *Now that I added auditory feedback on the 'Return', backspace, space bar, W, A, S, and D keys— plus the home row? I'll touch type even faster.*

The keyboard and laptop reunite, after waiting five minutes for Muta to return from their minute long break. Fingers splayed over the numpad, speeding through the key binds scrawled on their bare forearm. *Thank Arceus that I installed a clicky mechanical switch under the 'Return' key, like Paerce. I blew a day's pay on quieter ones before he stopped me...*

Switching to their desktop, they nod at their mouse cursor before planting it on their word processor... but then they reverse course.

PAULINE UGALDE

Shaking, they open Discord and barge into 'The Discyples,' their housemates and friends' server.

Category: School
#progress, (text channel)
How's your homework anxiety coming along?

Mutavault · Today at 6:50 PM
Have everything. But finishing my paper first. Polished but needs optimizing.
6:50 PM
@DaFirenze Thanks for the help.
6:50 PM
BTW the blue clicky switches feel great.

DaFirenze · Today at 6:50 PM
Anything to minmax you!

Mutavault ·Today at 6:50 PM
How are you?

DaFirenze ·Today at 6:50 PM
Speedrunning dinner.

Mutavault · Today at 6:50 PM
Is @Wavedash using TAS again?

8

THESIS

DaFirenze ·Today at 6:50 PM

No. But she performed a TAS of the route to this event.

6:51 PM

30 seconds faster if not more.

6:51 PM

She vaulted three Teslas—new record.

Mutavault · Today at 6:51 PM

👍👍👍 DUDE!!! Go on?

Category: General
#events, (text channel)
Where you're going, when, and why. Please spam us with updates!

Mutavault · Today at 6:51 PM

@DaFirenze @Wavedash is gonna be pissed you call her parkouring TAS.

DaFirenze · Today at 6:51 PM

It sure as hell looks like a computer's subbing in.

6:52 PM

Literally she ran on the front desk.

6:52 PM

And rolled under the barrier to cut the line.

Mutavault · Today at 6:52 PM

😨😨😨😨😨😨😨😨😨😨😨😨FUCKING HELL

DaFirenze · Today at 6:52 PM

Right!? She hasn't been this hyped since our Ghostface costumes came last year!

6:53 PM

But I don't blame Cydni. Journalism couldn't get enough chairs.

Mutavault · Today at 6:53 PM

That crowded?

DaFirenze · Today at 6:53 PM

EVERYONE'S HERE!

Wavedash · Today at 6:53 PM

There aren't 5000 people. 1500. Tops.

6:53 PM

Even that's a stretch.

6:53 PM

@DeFirenze You dumped your calculator in 2019. But even you know that.

DaFirenze · Today at 6:53 PM

@Wavedash 😊AND FUCK YOU TOO

Mutavault · Today at 6:53 PM

DaFirenze · Today at 6:53 PM

Wavedash · Today at 6:53 PM

BTW I didn't run on desks.

6:53 PM

I ran up that wall where we sit during Twitch streams.

6:54 PM

But not before Paerce claimed our spots. Some dudes almost stole them.

6:54 PM

They only saw when he was right behind them.

Mutavault · Today at 6:54 PM

HOT DAMN EZIO did you use a TAS too?

DaFirenze · Today at 6:54 PM

Hell no! I got to the cafeteria 90 seconds before Cydni today. 🤺

Wavedash · Today at 6:54 PM

This crowd's hyped. Even Medaelia's hyped.

PAULINE UGALDE

Mutavault · Today at 6:54 PM
You haven't called her hyped since she sent us The Summoning!

Wavedash · Today at 6:54 PM
Paerce bodied me. He finished the whole funky outro before I came.

Mutavault · Today at 6:54 PM
@Wavedash WORSHIP! 🙏
(Ultraliminal reacted with 🙏)

DaFirenze · Today at 6:54 PM
@Mutavault WORSHIP! 🙏
(Ultraliminal reacted with 🙏)
6:55 PM
She's still wants our This Place will Become Your Tomb and Missing Limbs hot takes.
(Ultraliminal reacted with 😊↕.)
6:55 PM
Of course she's hosting a Take Me Back to Eden listening party. Soon.
(Ultraliminal reacted with ◎)
(Ultraliminal reacted with ❤.)

Ultraliminal · Today at 6:55 PM
@DaFirenze PREPARE

THESIS

Mutavault · Today at 6:55 PM

Don't remind me I saved her scaryass Tiktoks about The Summoning. 😆

(Ultraliminal reacted with 🙏)

Wavedash · Today at 6:55 PM

(Wavedash/Cydni attaches a photo of a table on the isle and in the front of a crowded room. A six-foot wall to one side divides the room in half.

6:55 PM

(Cydni posts a link to a message from Ultraliminal/ Medaelia, in the Offerings voice channel, in the Music category: a screenshot from Spotify, displaying he aforementioned song.)

6:55 PM

LOL. Medaelia just linked it again. Five minutes out. LET'S DO THIS. WORSHIP 🙏

(Mutavault reacted with 🙏)

(DaFirenze reacted with 🙏)

(Ultraliminal reacted with 🙏)

Mutavault · Today at 6:55 PM

Good luck.

PAULINE UGALDE

Category: School
#progress (text channel)

Mutavault · Today at 6:55 PM
Editing time music's on LET'S FUCKING GO

DaFirenze · Today at 6:55 PM
Good luck. Text when you wanna come home.
6:56 PM
Even if it's at 3 AM. Again.

Wavedash · Today at 6:56 PM
Don't overexert yourself.
6:56 PM
We need you at the new house.

Mutavault · Today at 6:56 PM

6:56 PM
I can't guarantee I'll be done early.
6:56 PM
But I'll message when I'm done.
6:57 PM
Wait tell Kayleigh I'll be right back!

DaFirenze · Today at 6:57 PM
NO problem.

6:57 PM

@Pluribus Emery will make it—they didn't break the rules.

6:57 PM

You don't have to leave WoW.

Wavedash · Today at 6:58 PM

It's only 10 in Virginia. She's fine.

6:58 PM

@Pluribus Where's Hoffman and Schenk?

DaFirenze · Today at 6:58 PM

Are they working?

Pluribus · Today at 6:58 PM

Lex is @ a clients house

6:58 PM

She wont pick up

6:58 PM

Yeh patrick is here.

6:58 PM

But not r guild

PAULINE UGALDE

Category: General
#life, (text channel)
When everything isn't fine.

Mutavault · Today at 6:58 PM
@Pluribus No raid? But you waited since last year
to do one.

Pluribus · Today at 6:58 PM
No
6:58 PM
Since starting school again
6:58 PM
Since jan 6
6:58 PM
But they'll understand.
6:59 PM
Dr. Rees helped me form the guild.
6:59 PM
I do owe her.

Category: General
#events, (text channel)

Wavedash · Today at 6:59 PM
@Pluribus GET OVER HERE!

THESIS

Pluribus · Today at 6:59 PM
Yeh thats a bet
6:59 PM

Wavedash · Today at 6:59 PM
MORTAL KOMBAT!!!

DaFirenze · Today at 6:59 PM
Fuck it
7:00 PM
WE'LL BE YOUR fighting game main matchmakers after we're done moving in.

Before Muta begins editing, they wait for the beat drop from the song playing in their headphones. They allow themselves to jam out for one loop, making a genuine effort to hum along to the layered flute and theremin. Head nods keep pace with the hand drums, the main percussion instrument. The song introduces piano, but swaps instruments twice: Strings, followed by a banjo and baritone vocals. The last section of the song strips out all instruments except the hand drums and theremin. Muta gathers their reference materials, saving their draft for last.

When the song loops, Muta's fingers fly across

the keys, at the section of their thesis requiring the most revisions. They snipe spelling, grammar, and rhetorical mistakes, each section cleared motivating them to stand from their seat and pump their fists. The last sentence halts their progress, however. Skipping rereading time, they delete and replace the text.

By weaponizing—

They delete it and restart.

Because fans know the rules that characters must abide by in order to successfully survive a horror movie—

Again, they delete their conclusion and replace it.

Authors toy with fans' emotions—

They stop their music to shriek between clenched teeth. "How am I so shitty? I explained it perfectly to Dr. Engle!"

Muta knocks their chair over and slams their keyboard onto the desk; the sound jolts them back to attention. Their face and neck flush with their sudden burst of anger, before they sit back down, cringing in response to their behavior. They resume their music but don't nod along. Calmer but conflicted, Muta resumes typing, remaining still as each word appears. They only finalize the last sentence once they read it without reacting.

THESIS

Authors weaponize fans' horror and metanarrative knowledge, and fans immerse themselves in the ensuing emotional sacrifice.

They open the submission page for Media Studies Capstone—Dr. Renee Engle's class. Muta beams, as they enter their thesis' title: "Its Suffering was Real: Technology's Impact on Horror' Metanarrative Effectiveness." They check the time: Half-past eleven. *She won't mind that it's late.*

They reopen Discord and almost post in '*The Discyples,*' but instead, they draft an email. They set surrender to the urge to gush, to slip in a pop culture reference—or three.

Hi Renee,

Thanks so much for letting me submit my thesis past the deadline.

I have lots of assignments with clustered deadlines—I just finished Dr. Bates' paper last night. My friends and I are also moving into our new house on the 16th. But I wanted to give this paper the time it deserved. I needed a break—even if it was just a day.

And about our Experimental Film final? I'll forward a Dropbox link when I'm done. We're so happy you're interested in Morton's Lens.

If you want to download it using that link, the .

PAULINE UGALDE

zip password is:

    Buff3r3d_R3v3rs3d_W@v3d@sh

        Thanks for everything,
          Emery

Muta takes long drafts from one can of a soda they bought outside, minutes before entering the editing bay. Only after they've chased it with water do they read their only unread Discord messages: From Dr. Daniel Ison and Dr. Jason Bates. Their conversation occupies *The Discyples* from one P.M. onward, for half an hour.

Category: General
#life, (text channel)

    PhaseChanger · Today at 1:00 PM
    AHHHHH SHIT I'M NOT DONE WITH MY STUFF AHHHHHHHH

    Z3rosum · Today at 1:00 PM
    @PhaseChanger Daniel. Calm down. What's wrong?

    PhaseChanger · Today at 1:00 PM
    I'm not done with something I'm bringing to an on campus event tonight.

THESIS

Z3rosum · Today at 1:00 PM

Ya mean Dr. Rees' workshop?

PhaseChanger · Today at 1:00 PM

Z3rosum · Today at 1:01 PM

Can I call you? I know some mindfulness techniques. They'll work. Fast.

1:01 PM

For real. These aren't bullshit.

PhaseChanger · Today at 1:01 PM

My office hours don't start for another hour.

Z3rosum · Today at 1:01 PM

I don't have to come. Cydni and Paerce did this before tests.

1:01 PM

If you can visualize objects—you can do this one.

1:01 PM

Hell—I'll do it with you.

1:01 PM

Anything to withstand finals week.

Z3r0sum · Today at 1:25 PM
Feeling better?

PhaseChanger · Today at 1:25 PM
My heart's not beating out of my chest.

1:25 PM
But don't worry about me anymore go take care
of yourself.

Z3r0sum · Today at 1:25 PM
Way ahead of you.
1:25 PM
Medaelia ain't gonna be happy you're stressed—
but she'll appreciate the effort.
(PhaseChanger reacted with 😄)

Ultraliminal · Today at 1:25 PM
@PhaseChanger Is your artifact content
complete?
(PhaseChanger reacted with ☺ ↕ .)

PhaseChanger · Today at 1:25 PM
Of course 😰

Ultraliminal · Today at 1:25 PM
I will obtain whatever you lack. We will approach
its realization.

PhaseChanger · Today at 1:25 PM
Thank you. So much. 😊😊😊😊😊😊😊

Z3rosum · Today at 1:25 PM
I'm taking a Catharsis nap.
1:25 PM
You should too, Daniel. Don't spam me with water colors—they're awesome but please chill.
(PhaseChanger reacted with a 🛏)

Muta tears up at the exchange. They screenshot the post with the feather emoji and send it to Cydni with the caption 'He caved! He played *Celeste* since when 🎮' They snicker at Daniel's most recent posts.

Category: Fandom
#hyperfixation, (text channel)
What has got a taste for you?

Z3rosum · Today at 1:30 PM
@Mutavault I laughed at Kill Counting so hard I almost choked on my coffee.
1:30 PM
I don't know when we'll get to talk next. So I wanted to tell you I enjoyed it. A lot.

1:30 PM

You got me invested in horror game trends.

1:30 PM

And I'll definitely live tweet Morton's Lens.

PhaseChanger · Today at 1:30 PM

👍👍👍👍

1:30 PM

Sorry @Z3r0sum I have to.

[Daniel attaches multiple photos of a hardcopy version of Muta's paper for Jason's class: *Kill Counting*. Multicolored annotations fill the margins and between the blank lines in the double spacing. Drawings on the backs of the pages include a machete decapitating a zombie vertically, robed figures holding hunting knives and flip phones, and a six-person carousel with a shotgun pointed at it.]

Wavedash · Today at 1:31 PM

@PhaseChanger I love you Daniel but please delete those. We have a Gaming Spoilers channel.

[Cydni links to the Gaming Spoilers text channel, in the Spoilers category.]

DaFirenze · Today at 1:31 PM

@PhaseChanger @Z3r0sum Thanks for hyping us up BUT NO 😳

THESIS

The outlines of the art alone give Daniel's excitement away. Muta squeals, as they switch to his most recent barrage of messages, sent scattershot across multiple text channels.

**Category: General,
#milestones, (text channel)**
Personal, professional, nerd—but bring the receipts!

PhaseChanger · Today at 1:32 PM
[Daniel posts two screenshots: the first of a Steam game purchase, dated May 17, 2025, the second the detailing his total play time, as of June 10, 2024.]
1:32 PM
I procrastinated so hard? I finished Inscryption on Monday.
1:33 PM
Even just thinking about the ending makes me sad. But it gave me closure.
1:33 PM
@Mutavault @DaFirenze @Wavedash @Pluribus Thanks for the recommendation.

PAULINE UGALDE

Category: General
#shameless-plug, (text channel)
Exactly what it says on the tin. Promote yourself and others.

PhaseChanger · Today at 1:33 PM
[Daniel links back to his post in #milestones.]
1:33 PM
I have so much fanart!
1:33 PM
[Daniel attaches a collage of drawings, made on different sizes of paper, in pencil, adding hand-drawn elements to generative AI art, and ink colors that almost glow. File names include Creep.jpg, Alwayspickthis.png, and Jeanjacketbutpeople.jpg.]
1:33 PM
Yes I have more.
1:33 PM
@Mutavault @Wavedash @DaFirenze If you could make a short film honoring this game— Dana and I liked without even playing it? The least I could do was play the damn thing.
1:34 PM

THESIS

Relieved, Muta lays down the burden of moderating their Discord server. Their messages to their friends trip over each other to appear in the 'Milestones' text channel, misspellings and all.

Category: School
#completion, (text channel)
Show us your unlocks! And source lists!

Mutavault · Today at 11:40 PM
I'MDONEFUCKYEAH!!!
[They attach a screenshot of the successful assignment submission page for Media Studies Capstone.]
11:40 PM
🍸🍸🍸🍸

Category: School
#progress, (text channel)

Mutavault · Today at 11:40 PM
Editing Morton's Lens now. Cleanup but not too bad.
11:40 PM
HYPEASS MUSIC GO!!!

PAULINE UGALDE

Category: Music
#auxchord, (voice channel)
Play music that isn't an offering here.

> **Mutavault · Today at 11:40 PM**
> [Muta posts a link to a song called The Scrybe of Beasts, by Jonah Senzel.]
> **11:40 PM**
> 

A bit crushed, distorted version of the same boss music from before compels Muta to surrender to their intuition. When they remove bloated silence or tweak sound levels, they do so in rhythm with the music. *Shit—we did so good when replicating the bass. It was the best thing we've heard in years!*

Muta checks the submission time on their confirmation receipt for their Experimental Film project: Quarter past one.

Category: School
#completion, (text channel)

> **Mutavault · Today at 1:17 AM**
> FUCK YEAH I'M DONE!!!
> [They post their confirmation receipt for Dr. Dana Vega's Experimental Film class. The title of

THESIS

Muta's, Cydni's, and Paerce's experimental film group project reads, Morton's Lens.]

Category: General
#shameless-plug, (text channel)

Mutavault · Today at 1:17 AM
[Muta posts three links: a link to their post in Completion; the Morton's Lens Dropbox link; and a YouTube channel, also called The Discyples, where they've uploaded it.]
1:17 AM
@1stlight Hi Renee I sent you the .zip password with my paper. @everyone I'll send it to you on request.

Category: General
#events, (text channel)

Mutavault · Today at 1:17 AM
@DaFirenze @Wavedash Please pick me up. I'm in the first editing bay.
1:17 AM
@Pluribus Hello! I'm alive! In time for final move in day!
1:17 AM
Playing another run.

PAULINE UGALDE

Pumping their fist at the screen, Muta switches tabs to their current gaming session on their laptop, displaying the 'Continue' option in the main menu. The screen receives a fist bump, as authentic as a real person. *Fuck yeah, dude. We did it.*

2

STUDIO, KESS BUILDING, II

Muta wakes at a wooden table in near darkness. They don't even confirm if they have their phone or wallet. Instead, their head whips up off their folded arms and toward the pair of glowing, orange eyes, staring through them. "Fuck—not again!"

Their shouts die on their lips, curled in a gentle smile. Acoustic guitar arpeggios layered atop crackling, oscillating noise, play in their stalwart earphones. Their gaze gravitates to the upper right hand corner of their screen: It's three-thirty in the morning.

Rubbing sleep from their eyes, Muta stands, knocking their chair into the wall behind them with a bang, and pivots toward the ajar editing bay door. They unsling their messenger bag from their body and almost hurl it onto the table. Their fingers close over the golden strawberry pin secured to their breast pocket. *No mugging?*

They retrieve their phone and check their Discord messages. The last one they received occurred at seven P.M. The last messages they wrote two hours ago, but now, the app reads 'Message failed to send' next to each. Even the screenshot of their submission confirmation pages didn't send. They scroll backward; The same error notification appends to their posts proceeding midnight.

They read the app and diagnostic icons on their laptop and phone: Wi-fi is dead. Muta's phone has seventy-five percent battery, identical to when they entered the editing bay, over eight-and-a-half hours ago. They rummage through their messenger bag's pockets, alert for misplaced objects.

They find nothing.

At last, they notice an open tab, besides their game: A screenshot of its diagetic cursor hovering over the glitchy 'New game' option. The file's properties read: *Date modified: 6/12/2024, 7:00 PM.* In one corner, Muta's annotation, made with the tablet surface of their laptop screen, reads Cut this 7:15 PM. 'Enact' overlays the now struck through text.

Muta dons the camera bag at their feet, while calling out the editing bay door. "Hello?"

In spite of themselves, they flinch at the echo

of their own voice. Do they wait for a response in anticipation or fear? They take the well-trodden path down the hall to the equipment room, removing the camera from their shoulders, like dozens of—

They freeze a step outside the doorway. Grooves score the metal door, and the wall next to it, retracing the path they walked. The window at their eye level struggles to stay intact, as similar cracks web across it.

As they enter, almost every light sizzles above them, shattered. The room's contents blankets the floor, and even the walls and ceiling bear shrapnel. Horizontal gashes like knife wounds carve through wood, concrete, and metal. Muta digs a soda can from their bag, before hefting the entire stash in one hand: A bludgeon worthy of facing the end, too close at hand, alone.

Circumventing what they can, they wince as they crunch down on gear that their professors drilled in their head to treat with care. *An intruder broke in while I was playing.*

To one side, a piece of cloth stands out against the ground. Muta crawls toward a torn piece of fabric—

It's a blood-speckled shirt sleeve, marred with multiple slashes.

Muta stills and peers at the blood. Paerce's CSI

ramblings while watching the news, or while on of them sustained a phone call while traveling alone, sooth their nerves. *It's not clotted—it's less than eight—four?—hours old. I was asleep. There was a struggle, but the building stayed open. Someone was— They're looking for me.*

They're looking for me. They're looking for me. They're—

Muta shakes and hyperventilates. The stinging cuts, and racket of colliding with abandoned film gear, don't compel them to silence: Their exhaustion finally does.

They reevaluate the room and blood stains. From behind the ajar door: *Cydni and Paerce never came.*

Their friends' promises, made as they began their first year of college, ring in their head. *'Friends don't lie—and never split the party!'*

'Jesus Christ—you don't know the rules? There are certain rules! That one must abide by in order to successfully survive a college campus!'

'Okay, I'm drawing a line in the fucking sand here, do not read the Latin.'

Muta closes the door and switches the camera on. It's fully charged, not half full. They perform a white balance check, holding the supplied white index card in their free hand. Satisfied with their camera's color scheme, on one knee, they grasp a hollow, metal bar, a boom pole segment: A lapel microphone alternative on a film set. They push a second, shorter segment through their belt loops.

They salvage cloth and cables with their concealed multitool, when they aren't retrieving the plentiful pieces sliced apart gifted to them, already at natural fracturs or joints. Calculating the proportions by eye, they fashion a harness. It crisscrosses their chest, back, and shoulder. Camera mountings transmute into existence from mismatched clips. They even attach a makeshift swiveling arm to expand and refine the available camera angles on their chest.

When the rig passes the improvise stress tests initiated by their jittering fingers, Muta hurries—the resist every urge to expose their position by sprinting. They powerwalk back to the editing bay and pack up. *Until I call the cops—*

Until I'm safe enough to call the cops? I'm on my own.

Muta reconfigures their cross-body bag's straps, transforming it into a backpack. Pocketing their phone, they walk toward the film department exit, pricking up their ears—

The lights flicker, in the studio doubling as a classroom. They pivot toward it, confronted by bloody fingerprints on the doorframe, replicating downward facing claw marks. At their forehead height, a dripping, bloody handprint blocks most of the door's inset window.

A blood trail, inches from their feet, snakes toward the door. Even in the sparse light, it, and the blood on the door, almost shine. Crouching, they utilize their new harness to film each piece of evidence in succession, to zoom in on the blood trail. The sparse light reveals further horizontal score marks, in the walls and doors between their editing bay and the studio. The outer door handles, sliced in half and sheared off at their bases, glint against the tiled floor. None of the doors have an intact handle. Muta bends over, zooming in on the handles as close as possible without touching them, or the floor.

When they've finished, they open the door, while taking care to preserve the fingerprints.

Two steps inside, Muta turns their head, one inhale away from vomiting on their equipment. Only after waiting a few minutes—hours—do they look again, supporting themselves with the long boom pole, propped on the wall next to the door.

Professor Leslie Weaver, a man in his mid-forties with shorn hair, a dress shirt with one sleeve, and a gunshot wound. He sustained multiple gunshots to the chest, and at least one other gunshot to his right kidney. Leslie lies on the floor, inches away from Dana, a woman no more than five years his senior, in casual clothes, pointing a smartphone at her face. The whites of her remaining eye show. Blood streaks her right leg, from a jagged cut. A foot of gore smeared linoleum floor separates her right foot and the stump of her ankle.

People have ten—twelve—pints of blood. This cut bled at least ten pints!

Does Muta cry, or imagine Dana's agony vividly enough to share in her pain? Teeth clenched, stomach churning, and curiosity overtaking them, they free the phone from Dana's rigor mortis grip.

I can't contaminate a crime scene if I'm killed...

Dana's phone, open to the most recent item in the camera app, displays a video... half an hour old.

3

STUDIO, III

Bleeding from multiple fresh and bound wounds, PROFESSOR DANA VEGA crouches behind the studio door, shaking. Blood clings to, and drips from, her clothes and hair. She takes ragged breaths, and her phone shakes in her hand. Even so, she keeps her face in focus.)

DANA

Emery? Sorry if this is Razzie-worthy.

(The phone's lens wobbles to focus on her nostrils for an instant, but she corrects it.)

DANA

3 AM. June 13. 2024.

(DANA peeks around the door, before extending one arm beyond the edge to pan the camera around the room. Like the equipment storage area, the classroom's shattered furniture and gear impale every available surface. The debris' breakage points also follow natural joints, and fractures also follow clean, straight lines. Blood obscures the room's threshold.)

DANA

My phone will say that. I don't know the real time.

(She cocks her head outside, toward a metallic crash.)

DANA

I'm Dana Vega. Film professor. Renewal University.

(The video buffers or skips forward , whenever doors bang open and close. Freeze frames of DANA gaping at her surroundings flash onscreen.)

Muta rewinds Dana's footage; the playback issues persist. As the anomalies occur, the video's timestamp doesn't freeze; it advances. Muta flicks through the apps list in Dana's settings, laps the room, and finds no third-party editing software or intact computers.

There aren't devices to edit this in post—so *what the hell?*

THESIS

DANA (*mouthing*)
No...

(*DANA squeezes her eyes shut briefly.*)

DANA
I'm being stalked by my colleague—Leslie—he's
killed multiple people. He's brainwashed.

(*The lights overhead and in the hallway, tinted red,
flicker in erratic patterns.*)

DANA
The staff is too. My students have proof.

(*More crashing sounds and localized video anomalies
overlap her words.*)

DANA
The students are safe. But he knows I'm here.

(*DANA stands. She pulls a necklace out from under her
collar: a stylized film roll, canister and all. She unrolls it.
Images flashing in succession, like an inserted montage,
overtake MUTA'S vision, enabling full screen on a video.
An approaching crowd covered in blood with white
eyes. A woman strangling a man from behind, tattoos*

modeling her hands. A man, clenching a chain around his neck, stares down at two mangled bodies, positioned mid leap, as if each began shielding the other. Quarter-sized, transparent patches fill the centers of his palms. A voice accompanies the last rapid fire vision.)

CYDNI (*voiceover*)
The lone wolf dies. But the pack survives.

(DANA zooms in on the film roll, which stores the same images.)

Muta rewinds the video: no montage appears.

(DANA stops on one frame of a stylized, impaled eye. While tracing the borders of the frame, her free hand mimes grasping a knife. The film stock perforates and separates. She drops the film roll beside her and grips the frame.)

DANA
Not even a double tap killed him.

(As DANA speaks and films the hallway outside, freeze frames of her leaping out from behind a corner, arm raised as if wielding a gun, flash past Muta's eyes. She *mimes shooting LESLIE six times, bangs and all. During the first, LESLIE clutches his chest with both hands. His head jars back, and he collapses. Blood pours between his fingers and through his palm holes. LESLIE stalks into view, his bawled fists throttling a pair of glinting typewriter spools. An ink ribbon feeds between them. He doesn't react to her.)*

DANA
Tell. Everyone. Don't blame
yourself—your friends didn't... Don't.

(LESLIE enters.)

DANA
Because sacrifices must be made.

(LESLIE'S silver eyes target DANA. She zooms the camera in on her right eye, also colored silver. She doesn't resist, as he swings the outstretched Gigli saw at her stomach. She stumbles, her hands cradling her phone, even as she sprawls on her back. LESLIE kneels, coiling and tightening the makeshift garrote around her right foot. An impossible amount of blood gushes onto the floor and his hands. As DANA's dismembered foot slides away from her ankle, she mimes stabbing and twisting a knife in her right

eye, as if extracting it. LESLIE'S punctured right eye bleeds aqueous and vitreous humor. He releases her and falls next to her. The necklace and Gigli saw crumble.)

4

LOBBY, IV

Muta's knees buckle. As Leslie enters the room in the video, they bow their head, sobbing into their jacket and sitting in between their professors, a hand resting on each of their chests. Neither the blood from Leslie's manifested gunshot wounds, nor Dana's ten—twelve—pints of sacrifice—deters them. Once their tears run dry, fear puppets them, so they neither withdraw from the gore, nor look away.

Sickened by their lingering desire to know, they palm Dana's phone again. They AirDrop the video to themselves and unclip the camera from their chest, knuckles bleached white. *Only I know they're dead.*

Starting with Leslie, they reexamine both bodies. They take his photo.

Muta returns Dana's phone, forcing

themselves to look at her mangled, bloody corpse. *I can't look away but I can't whitewash this either. I want this to be the perfect memento of her.*

They take her photo.

Rising, they exit the studio, shutting the door behind them and switching off the light. Camera and phone imprinting into their ear and skull, Muta accepts the AirDrop request and calls 911.

"We're sorry. The number you have dialed is not in service at this time."

Muscle memory saves their phone from a suicidal fall and works the camera. Their fingers numb, as they lower it and turn toward the exit door. They zoom in on their screwed up face, their summary stuck in their throat. *This is hard news, your last words.*

"I'm Muta Davila. Kess building. Renewal University. I found Professors Dana Vega and Leslie Weaver dead in the studio. Dana explained how she got there on film."

Their breath hitches. "She wanted me to tell everyone.

"I'm alone.

"The police can't come since 911's dead."

Muta enters the hall connecting the film department to the building beyond. They rattle a vending machine as they pass. Setting down the camera, they shake it harder. The contents cascade into the tray. They grin, stowing snacks and the few remaining bottles of their favorite soda, before entering the lobby.

The man's spine, bent backward, doesn't obscure his face. Bracing themselves, they permit themselves to wail once, before covering their mouth and homing in on Daniel's body. They don't wretch or look away. Shaking, they cross the lobby and round the body to face him. He lies inside, feet touching the doormat, his posture implying a sprint. His ribs protrude out of his chest and through his vest, and his blood saturates his dress shirt and the floor beneath him. Muta's jaw falls open. "Why?" Muta whispers over him.

Focusing the camera on Daniel's face, mouth set in an unwavering line, even in death, Muta cups their chin in thought. They glance out the glass doors at a silent campus.

The whirring of cars speeding by doesn't fade in and out. Lights from the outdoor walkways or students' dorms don't twinkle. The chilled drink in their bag, however, hacks away at their complacency, weighing down their body, flesh, and bone, until they confirm its frosted surface for themselves.

It's all they can do to transfer the camera to their improvised chest harness, and avoid tripping over themselves, while rushing out the door. Muta shines their phone flashlight on the ground, scrutinizing the cobblestone path to the wider campus. They film the thickest trail, and multiple thinner ones, which start where the university's main concrete walkway transitions to cobblestone, stopping at the lobby. Only Ison's trail crosses the threshold. It coagulates more than Leslie's shirt.

Their jaw drops. The camera shakes so hard that it unbuckles from the harness. They catch it in time but continue their train of thought.

Daniel died before Dana but after I fell asleep.

Returning to Daniel, they haul his body off the floor, just enough to point his soles out the door, toes touching the floor. They pan the camera along the line of sight formed by his blank eyes, then drop his body.

"You coordinated with Dana. One of you would warn me. The other would protect them."

Bluntly, to the camera: "Leslie chased and killed Daniel. Then Dana."

Muta gestures at his broken body and writes multiple Ls in the air. "And campus security—police—"

They gape at his vest: It's not fabric. Instead, panels of pads of note paper, open notebooks, and even square sticky note pads, adhere to a duct tape frame. Instead of wilderness or urban survival gear, drawing and writing implements slot into MOLLE compatible webbing circumventing the vest. A matching belt straddles his waist, bandoliers bursting with drawings hanging from it. Pouches of paper adorn the belt. One pouch, its flap hanging open next to Daniel's belt buckle. They open it, the glowing contents visible even through the duct tape walls.

The top page contains a recreation of Paerce's rough sketch of his, Muta, and Cydni's celebratory graduation tattoo: Three downward, diverging arrows with a shared stem. Its ink almost glows blue and green in the darkness. Beneath, layers of art represent diverse styles. Tracings of preexisting objects, and composites of generative AI images with Daniel's additions, coexist. They marvel at the color palette, which even persists in the MOLLE vest and belt. Pen strokes of glowing ink dye the makeshift cloth over Daniel's chest and the pouches flanking the belt buckle.

After reverting back to handheld filming, they shoot each page with their camera and phone, lingering on their friend group's sketch. They conclude by taking Daniel's photo.

Muta shrugs and seizes the sketch. "I can't contaminate a crime scene if I'm in it."

They tuck it into the innermost pocket of their

bag, where they conceal their passport and emergency cash. "I'd say if I die, give my stuff and this footage to Paerce Morrissey, Cydni Sorrell... and Kayleigh Lamar...

"But there's no way in hell I'm dying before the next election."

They unbuckle Daniel's belt and sling it around their own waist, notes and all, and lower the man's vest over their head. Before leaving the building, Muta captures the steadiest closeup of their pin as they can, removing residual blood with their sleeve, and secure the camera to their shoulder. They scan the nearby campus, a route already forming before their mind's eye. As they reassure themselves, their lucid tone surprises them. The mantra Cydni recites before she, Paerce, or Muta practice *Celeste* speed runs sprints through their anxiety, like Madeline summitting a room.

"This is it, Emery. Just Breathe. You can do this."

5

LOBBY, ADMISSIONS BUILDING, I

Memories of Muta's playthroughs of *The Last of Us*, *Celeste*, and *Mirror's Edge* resurface, life preservers on a panic ocean. They leverage rubble as cover and harness their momentum via parkour, shortening their route to conserve energy. They climb walls that either supported campus buildings, or that combatants or survivors—

Assuming that anyone survived.

Blood paints the pavement and wrecked walls. Most retain fresh blood's coloration, even after hours of supposed oxygenation—

Blood isn't the only source of the red coloration.

Dotted, red lines blink into existence as Muta looks. The lines sharpen, not dull, on film. They smile, as the line snakes ahead of them, along the top of and down the far side of a nearby wall. As they jump off the wall and pull themselves over it, serene words hide beneath their footfalls. Paerce's voice resonates as clearly as if he was above them.

His voice echoes the first time he detailed parkour methodology for their collective college friend group. He made good on this method, by scaling the front all of their lower division dorm.

His voice ascends ahead of them, following the red line and fading with distance. "We call ourselves runners."

An audio icon in the corner of the camera's display blinks: It records the sound. "We exist on the edge between the gloss and reality, the mirror's edge."

Muta follows. Though taxing, they optimize the camera's field of view. They take special care to attain full coverage when performing maneuvers like vaulting obstacles or negotiating tight spaces. In a flash of inspiration, they grab a brick from scattered rubble: A diversion or emergency bludgeoning weapon. However, they set it back down. *It's too large and dense. The full soda cans do it better.*

What building was this?

They crane their neck, until they pick out the

outline of an amphitheater. Somehow, it's intact, besides burn marks and debris impaled in cushions. Hardened, brittle, melted glass—a substance that resembles glass but isn't clear—paints the stage. *Dragon glass? Obsidian.*

Obsidian flows over the former stage and wings in broad strokes. An obsidian crater invades the primary backstage area, where Paerce worked. The bottom glows, even at a distance.

Muta gasps without muffling their voice. They run their hands over their face and arms, monitoring their breathing, tensing, wrestling back their urge to flee. *How many hours do I have until I taste metal? Until I start vomiting blood? Until my skin sluffs off?*

Instead of succumbing to their instincts, they dredge up the briefest description they can think of, zooming in on the glowing glass: "Radiation poisoning."

From then on, they describe their surroundings and announce their imminent route. They accompany each phrase with a pan or tracking shot across the landscape. They note the date, time, and notable events in a safe location every few minutes in a hushed, clear tone.

Muta leaves notes on the walls, or stashes scraps of paper beneath rocks or in crevices. They scrape messages in the dirt with their boom pole. Each time, they record shoulder mounted film footage and take photographs with their phone. Shadows of writing appear on these same surfaces, dates and times written in a wavering hand. Fractures in smaller obsidian deposits form mathematical symbols. Whenever they strain to read them better, the numbers vanish.

At sunrise, they gawk at the admissions building's lobby. The door's upper half clings to the wall. Its bottom half hangs off its hinges, jutting forward. As they judge the distance, the debris scattered between the entrance and a former wall serving as cover, Muta's thumbs and index fingers twitch and rock at waist height, mimicking inputs on a game controller. Feet away, a pixilated figure dashes toward and up the wall hiding Muta, interrupting the ascent by kicking off of it one body length off the ground. Instead of succumbing to gravity, the figure flies abreast with the wall, faster than when it began.

About one body length from the top, the figure reorients so it jumps off the wall, its soles grazing the concrete. Somehow, it boosts over the wall's topmost corner, in motion and speed, even while it traverses a straight path through the debris.

The figure ultra dashes down the wall and toward the door, each short hop and slide repetition in the chain compounding its speed. Its red hair flashes white whenever it touches the ground.

Muta jolts in confusion, as they wrestle with their hands. *How? I play on keyboard. Not—*

The figure's movements sync up with the mock controller inputs. Muta squints at their footage: Instead of a pixelated figure, Cydni demonstrates a speed run route to the door.

Muta shakes out their fingers. As blood flow returns, they sprint up and jump off of the wall, roll on landing using their unburdened shoulder, and flatten their profile to slide across the gap. They enter—

An impact jars their legs. They fall sideways, their head and camera missing—

They look around.

A couple feet beyond the doorway, the floor inclines and declines in quick succession. Similar formations crisscross every surface. On all fours, Muta raises one hand to their face: The nearest ridge cut their palm as they broke their fall. They crawl onward, camera first, ignoring their pain. They breathe, "I swear this isn't fake…."

A trail of blood, one handspan wide, starts on the floor, inches from their face, continuing beneath them and out the door. Sitting up, they attach the camera to their shoulder and position it to record their steps. They return to the spot where they noticed it and press onward, stopping in the center of the room, a man's upper body, from the rib cage up, divides a circle in half, made of his arms and legs, dismembered at the joints. Circular holes drill through his throat and chest. His intact fingers still wield a baton and taser, and an almost blood logged security badge dangles from his neck.

A woman Muta's age lies askew next to the man, arms spread, as if shoved aside. She's more than gutted like a fish. An unbroken line bisects her, from her pelvis to her sternum, including her underlying internal organs and vertebrae. Her dislocated and fractured arm and leg bent in the opposite direction from normal.

Feet away from the first two bodies, a woman in her late thirties lies face-up with a circular hole punched out of her body, where her heart would be. It lacks the segment of her spine that would have comprised the circle's diameter, and the surrounding muscle and organs. She clutches a metal compass on a chain wound around her wrist. Light shines through the transparent holes in her palms.

Transfixed, Muta tugs the compass out of her body with a squelch and wrestles with her hand—

Their thumb passes through her palm and emerges on the other side, devoid of gore.

Steeling themselves, they break her knuckles on her thumb, index, and middle fingers, and worm the compass out, grunting with the effort. They detach it from her wrist. Compass in one hand, camera in the other, they zoom in.

The compass' first, pointed arm, the fulcrum, tapers off to a sharp point for planting the compass onto the drawing surface. A writing utensil secures to the arm with a clamp, its width controlled by an attached screw. A second screw, with a nut threaded onto it, splays the hinge, comprised of the arms, open.

They rub their eyes, memories of bitching at Cydni in high school while struggling through homework welling back up. *How did I survive geometry without stabbing holes?*

They freeze and gape at the ceiling.

Muta slams the compass onto the nearest ridge and turns the nut: The arms don't straddle the ridge any tighter. When they turn the nut the opposite way, the arms loosen. Where they fit without empty space or slack, the semicircular protractor, bolted to the hinge, reads ninety degrees. They place the pen's tip and the fulcrum on each of the man's stab wounds. The ninety-degree angle bridges both wounds without exceeding either. Muta fine tunes the camera so one of the shielding woman's knees fills the frame. The disfigured joint matches the compass.

Muta repeats the same L-shaped motions that they performed in the communication building's lobby, drawing right triangles in the air: Identical to the interlocked metal pieces comprising the woman's wrist chain. The hypotenuse of each triangle acts as the longest straight side of the next one. The compass clipped onto the largest triangle.

Muta glares at the woman. "Daniel went out of his comfort zone for me—months after I took his class." Tears fall unabated. "You took him past the edge."

Muta doesn't turn the camera away. Instead, they heft it in one hand. The compass raised in a reverse grip, Muta stabs the geometry professor's blank eyes once—twice—thrice—then hurls it as hard as they can, so it impales into the ceiling. They don't flinch at the noise. They film the act with equal precision and stability as their parkour route through campus. They even immortalize their indignation. They shoot coverage of her body in as much detail as Dana and Leslie.

They don't suppress their shaking in fury as

they film her two kills, either. They cobble together a lighting rig, using their phone's flashlight and the floor ridges, obtaining legible footage of everyone's name tags, even Dr. Lyle Parr's.

They don't hide their repulsion, as they take one last long shot photo of each person before moving on.

6

SECURITY OFFICE, ADMISSIONS BUILDING, II

Wedging the long boom pole under their arm like a hiking stick, Muta navigates the rest of the lobby. Camera mounted on their shoulder, they push the back door open, scanning the offices' name plates.

The security office—someone's inside.

Muta presses their back against the wall. Peeking around the corner, they scrutinize a man, sitting upright and still, facing away from the door. He's disheveled, but not covered in excess blood: his own, or someone else's. The man searches the room, his movements and line of sight stable.

Muta wields the boom pole like a hammer and aims the camera down the hall. *After taking a few arrows to the knee and slashing the brachial artery? I don't need to double tap.*

Sidestepping against the wall, they turn the corner and duck into the nearest empty room, delaying looking away from him as long as possible. Behind the ajar door, they affix the camera to their chest instead of their shoulder. The lens points up at a slight incline from the horizontal: The perfect angle for recording the opposing man's face. They leave the office, arm themselves with both boom poles, and size up their attacker through the window.

Against their better judgment, Muta gasps. "Camerin?"

Bounding toward the office door, they smother their voice with their sleeve and halt midstride. Muta knocks on the door's inset window with the long boom pole, the shorter one raised in a reverse grip, at the man's eye level. *If he doesn't act like himself? I'll give him a painless death.*

Professor Camerin Romero faces them. A silver sheen ripples across his eyes, accentuating the bruises and bags underneath. Clothes torn and bloody, face and arms scarred, he doesn't hide his relief. However, instead of opening the door, he offers a pencil, impaling a blank sheet of paper: An improvised white flag.

Muta can't help but laugh. Camerin's laugh rings out as clearly as if he was doing so in their ear.

They enter the office and untie the camera, but it floats away and swivels. Fists bawled at his sides, Camerin turns his palms up at chest height, the camera obeying his twitching fingers. He nods once.

Overtaken by joy, Muta shifts in place, waiting for the camera to tilt, capturing both of them from head to toe. Romero retreats as Muta spreads their arms for a hug. Regardless, they sigh in relief, "Thank Arceus."

Camerin hesitates before approaching. "Thank Sinnoh," he corrects, smiling at the ground.

Muta restarts the hug; Camerin wrestles with his own body, to hold still in their arms. They push a chair up against the closed door, beneath the knob. The camera cradles into their shoulder, as they unseal the news valve: "Leslie Vernon killed Dana Vega in the studio."

"Dr. Lyle Parr killed Professor Daniel Ison in the Kess lobby."

"She died by murder-suicide just outside."

They shake again. "Dana told me..."

Muta sinks to the floor. Calculating the ideal distance, relative to their boom pole lengths, Camerin sits in front of them. He screws the cap over the camera lens partway, but Muta pries off his hand and fine tunes the angle. They shoot him in profile, even while blinded by their tears.

PAULINE UGALDE

Unblinking, Camerin loops one bracelet around his left thumb, forefinger, and middle finger, curling those fingertips toward each other, holding an imaginary pen. He mimes a scrawled sketch across his thigh, halting when he completes the stem and the outermost branching arrows in Daniel's notes. Muta's sobs cease. Mouthing, "Tell. Everyone," his right index finger hovers between his right eyelids. Muta gapes.

Resigned, he points to the unconscious screens behind him. Muta faces the nearest one, and Camerin sits behind them. They relinquish the camera, which tilts down to Camerin's hands. Bracelets of braided computer cables, bare wire, and paper adorn his wrists. He unties and joins them across his palms. Frowning in concentration, his curled fingers enclose the rope.

Camerin drapes the rope over Muta's shoulder, slashes his fingers through the air: He cuts Muta off before they can copy him. Instead, he rearms them, unhindered by their surprised recoiling. Static blooms across the screen. Camerin doesn't reapply the strip until Muta cracks their closed eyes open again. Muta squints at his approving nod, visible on the inside of their eyelids.

7

CAFETERIA, I

DR. MEDAELIA REES, *a Black woman in her early thirties, presides over a diverse, packed audience of faculty, staff, and journalism students. She draws on her hands and arms, atop tattoos, with a metal, dagger-shaped pen. Lengthwise sliders toggle her ink color. Wearing earbuds and sending rapid fire Discord posts, she sets a handwritten, multicolored flyer at each seat. Across the room, two seniors: PAERCE, a Black man, and CYDNI, an Asian woman, in matching outfits, lean on the cafeteria's dividing wall. PAERCE jots notes on his forearm and hand, before opening Discord. While CYDNI taps his shoulder camera mounting, she films MEDAELIA in profile.)*

CYDNI

It's hella packed but don't worry.
Jason and Renee made it—

PAULINE UGALDE

(*PAERCE shakes his head, angles his arm, evading CYDNI grasping for the hem of his sleeve.*)

PAERCE

I can't waste paper—time—

(*He opens his notepad. Reminders and 3D-print sketches crowd the pages. CYDNI cuts through the crowd; PAERCE motions silently, cluing her in to MEDAELIA'S actions. As Discord notifications ping, they enter the Offerings voice channel. MEDAELIA'S current Spotify song plays automatically. Beneath her first post, the Spotify screenshot, she posts a playlist code. They snicker at the name, Pre-Lecture Ritual. MEDAELIA circles her free hand in time with the music.*)

PAERCE

Our next commissions' shipping
when finals week ends.
No way in hell I'm holding Medaelia up!
This item's sick!

(*PAERCE jabs CYDNI's arm. Alone at a table, DR. JASON BATES, a man in his mid-30s, stands from his seat, pen in hand and a notebook open in front of him. He swats his short, brown hair out of his eyes and consults notes, also on his hand and forearm. He spreads his arms and*) beckons to PAERCE and CYDNI; PAERCE vaults the nearest table with one hand to enter the hug first.)

JASON

What happened!? You look like shit!

(PAERCE laughs. JASON offers his seat to him, but PAERCE shakes his head.)

JASON

Please don't push yourselves too hard...

(CYDNI laughs as she passes filming duties to PAERCE. She touch types her Discord messages.)

CYDNI

Jason? Emery would kill us if we did.

(She smiles. PAERCE gawks at his Quantitative Research Methods professors' appearance.)

PAERCE

But how about you? What's all that?

(JASON glances down at his notes, at the nearby, chatting professors, and MEDAELIA last.)

PAULINE UGALDE

PAERCE

I'm having fun—don't worry. I'm not.

(He pokes JASON'S inked forearm: the professor sneaks a peek at MEDAELIA again.)

PAERCE

You've got this. You and Renee survived
stabbing yourselves in the face!

(JASON at once drops his pen and laughs. He beckons them toward the journalism students packing the front row. He nods at CYDNI's camera: it's connected to her smartphone, strapped to her forehead.)

JASON

I can't stop you from streaming—but
you should pay for Kayleigh.

(CYDNI hands JASON an earbud. The Discyples' Events text channel updates in real time. KAYLEIGH spreads her arms in an embrace. JASON reciprocates.)

KAYLEIGH

I'm not that cheap! Schenk would
fuck me up if he knew.

THESIS

JASON

Even Renee knows you wouldn't
get home safe if you didn't pay up.

(Again, JASON beckons his students onward. He dabs sweat off his face as they walk away. PAERCE stops at a table in the second row. RENEE ENGLE, a woman in her early fifties, stands up. CYDNI mounts the camera on her shoulder while she and PAERCE embrace her.)

RENEE

You sure it was okay to leave Emery alone?

(The two friends laugh, followed by KAYLEIGH, after negligible lag.)

KAYLEIGH

They're kicking ass tonight. They're making
Alexandra Roivas look stupid!

(PAERCE retakes the camera and sits down. RENEE grins.)

PAERCE

After COVID? Sydney Prescott's
a wimp by comparison.

PAULINE UGALDE

(PAERCE hands CYDNI the index card, an inverted V when upright, marking her seat. The handwritten, multicolored text denotes her name and journalism major. He presents her and RENEE his card: alongside his name and theater major, it bears the same occupation, 'Fandom Actualization (Etsy)'. He and KAYLEIGH fist bump, as he unfolds a third card with her name, political science major and media studies minor, and identical job role. RENEE indicates MEDAELIA, who fixates on CYDNI's camera rig.)

RENEE

I don't want her to fuck you up.

PAERCE

She won't.

(KAYLEIGH turns around and points out her open bedroom door.)

KAYLEIGH

Schenk tased a treasonous fuck
insurrectionist. He can take her.

(PAERCE and CYDNI jab their thumbs at MEDAELIA. RENEE squeezes CYDNI's shoulder, as she takes her seat. MEDAELIA removes her earbuds, straightens, and raises

THESIS

her arms. Conversation fades. CYDNI erects her phone
on a telescoping stand, at KAYLEIGH'S seat.)

KAYLEIGH (*into the hall*)
It's live! Time to figure out what's on this thing …

(*PAERCE finds the next blank page in his notepad. He,
CYDNI, and KAYLEIGH stop updating MUTA.*)

MEDAELIA
Good afternoon…

(*The crowd responds neither uniformly nor in unison.*)

PAERCE and **CYDNI** (*after a slight delay*)
Good afternoon?

KAYLEIGH
Hello?

MEDAELIA
Have you've abandoned all notions of time?

KAYLEIGH
LOL?

(*The crowd laughs. CYDNI and PAERCE cheer.*

PAULINE UGALDE

MEDAELIA is undeterred, as she absorbs the awkward answers and chuckles to herself. She pinpoints and smiles at her students among the spectators, and winks at CYDNI's phone. KAYLEIGH flashes a thumbs up.)

CYDNI (*whispering*)
My emails at three A.M. about
catching birds in space were that... obvious?

PAERCE
I spelled Ezio's last name wrong
in my paper. Of course they were!

MEDAELIA
Or perhaps good evening is more fitting, Ms. Lamar?
Mr. Schenk?

(MEDAELIA approaches KAYLEIGH'S camera. Shaking, but maintaining steady eye contact, KAYLEIGH returns MEDAELIA'S wave with one hand, while zooming in on MEDAELIA'S face with the other, just offscreen. A chair creaks from that direction.)

KAYLEIGH
I'm paying—I stamp! The receipt's here!

(MEDAELIA winks with her right eye.)

THESIS

MEDAELIA

Your ability to pay—and remote attendance don't matter to me. Instead?

(*MEDAELIA walks past a cringing CYDNI to CAMERIN'S table. He shifts under her stare.*)

MEDAELIA

May I?

CAMERIN

W-w-what?

(*MUTA'S friends nod at each other and stifle giggles, as he works his jaw. MEDAELIA kneels beside him, ignoring the nearest empty chair next to him. KAYLEIGH'S posture relaxes.*)

CAMERIN

May I what?

(*She homes in on his bracelets. CAMERIN surrenders them, sighing in relief behind her. She stands on the empty chair, one in each hand above her head. CYDNI zooms in on the writing on the paper strands and turns her phone, giving KAYLEIGH full coverage. PAERCE scribbles notes.*)

PAULINE UGALDE

PAERCE

CAMERIN—!? What the hell? The Necronomicon—

(CYDNI shakes her head.)

CYDNI

No. HTML, dates. They're forum posts.

(PAERCE holds the flyer still to avoid crinkling, to avoid catching MEDAELIA'S attention. A technicolor, spoked diagram, labeled with departments at the Renewal University, superimposes over a grid of interlocking triangles inside a circle. CYDNI shoots coverage of the four quadrants of the crowd around them. JASON, eyebrows raised, leans in toward the cabling.)

MEDAELIA

Camerin? This is exactly what I wanted.

(He flinches as MEDAELIA returns his bracelets and paces in the center aisle, fidgeting with her pen.)

CAMERIN

It's nothing. Compsci gave me the cables—

(MEDAELIA cuts him off.)

THESIS

MEDAELIA
Who?

(*CAMERIN glances around. He waves at DR. JIM ASH, a computer science professor in his mid-forties, sitting at the table closest to door. He reciprocates. He lifts a flexible VR display off his face to wink at CAMERIN with each eye.*)

MEDAELIA
Don't be humble. I requested that each professor bring an... artifact, Embodying their field. For themselves and others.

(*MEDAELIA pivots toward DR. ELLISON JETT and her elaborate, woven wire necklace. She looks down.*)

MEDAELIA
This is my invitation given form.

(*ELLISON fumbles with the clasps at the back of her neck.*)

MEDAELIA
Can you assist me while showcasing that? Or perhaps, do so yourself?

PAULINE UGALDE

(DR. JANE WEST, *a chemistry professor with geometric, temporary tattoos on her forearms, stands from across the room and whoops.*)

JANE
You got this!

(*MEDAELIA glances toward the noise before ELLISON does, who hands the necklace off without prompting. MEDAELIA lifts the necklace above her head, as KAYLEIGH motions with her head for CYDNI to zoom in on the tattoo surrounding MEDAELIA'S right eye. Chains, impaled by spikes, form radiating triangles. The tattoo's color flows in real time.*)

KAYLEIGH
Hot damn! Huh!?

MEDAELIA
Tell us everything. For most of you are unaccustomed
to crafting such fine work—under duress, no less.

(*ELLISON blushes. MEDAELIA smiles back. PAERCE holds CYDNI's hands steady and refines her closeups on the necklace.*)

THESIS

MEDAELIA

I requested authenticity. Not artistry.
But it seems many of you—

(She points at JANE'S tattoos. CYDNI stops what she's doing and takes photos. Pins and stickers on her body cam harness and clothes mimic JANE'S designs.)

MEDAELIA

Were inspired.

(Her gaze snaps to PROFESSOR DAVIES RENNIE, also sitting at ELLISON'S table. He salutes. He's wearing layered, paper vambraces. PAERCE and CYDNI grin at his artifact. KAYLEIGH gapes, pinching herself.)

KAYLEIGH

By Senzel!

CYDNI

Did he copy our midterm?

(MEDAELIA produces an index card, folded lengthwise, from her jacket pocket, filled with her name. Under the cafeteria's white, fluorescent lights, the ink shifts colors.)

MEDAELIA
Record your findings on the reverse side.

(*She draws a purple, double-sided arrow between a stylized pause button and volume controls on the card's reverse side, inside a pair of Ɐ for all logic symbols. PAERCE hands a metal pen to CYDNI: It's a miniaturized version of MEDAELIA'S. Its body glows faintly purple. PAERCE streaks it across his palm: the ink matches the pen's and MEDAELIA'S ink's shade. He flashes his palm to KAYLEIGH, who adjusts her laptop's screen's brightness and contrast settings.*)

KAYLEIGH
Of course she's a blacksmith now—and
a metalhead... .

MEDAELIA
Share your findings with your colleagues:
alike and disparate.

(*She arcs her pen and arm across the room and reactivates her earbuds. Uneven, small group discussions begin in the crowd. Headbanging, she emerges from behind her table. As he works, PAERCE initiates the playlist using one of CYDNI's earbuds' touch controls, grinning. He and MEDAELIA mouth*

THESIS

along to the next song, 'Like That', also by Sleep Token.)

MEDAELIA

Trapped under the surface of your words... .

CYDNI beelines toward JANE, while PAERCE mounts the camera on his shoulder and her phone on his forehead. He scribbles notes, as CAMERIN twists his bracelets.)

ELLISON

Well shit! She's intense—

(PAERCE snickers into his hand. CAMERIN and DAVIES look up.)

ELLISON

No wonder her students love her. She...

(ELLISON clasps her hands on the table.)

ELLISON

She'll teach you how to use the tools,
to help yourself.

(PAERCE nods repeatedly. CAMERIN and DAVIES follow.)

PAULINE UGALDE

ELLISON
But she doesn't tolerate bullshit.

(*PAERCE pumps his fist. He waves at CYDNI, who films using his chest-mounted camera. She returns his long-distance fist bump. Static flashes across MUTA'S vision, as the point of view switches to CYDNI, shaking her head at JASON.*)

CYDNI
Why didn't you write your Discord handle?

(*JASON stabs toward RENEE with the pen offered by MEDAELIA.*)

RENEE
Letting Dr. Rees message you at will is unwise—
interesting, but unwise…

(*JASON shrugs.*)

JASON
It can't be worse than Emery's late night emails—
even you know this.

(*RENEE nods slowly as CYDNI slips between two tables to interview JANE. The designs temporarily tattooed on JANE'S forearms draw a grin out of CYDNI.*)

THESIS

CYDNI
Wait—you're serious?

(*JANE laughs. She sets a flat, water, fire, shock, and blast-proof case on the table, unlatching it to reveal paints and brushes of varying lengths and thicknesses.*)

JANE
Alchemists were scientists and artists.
But I didn't want diagrams.

(*MEDAELIA passes CYDNI, unnoticed. She traces her facial tattoo with her pen, INCLUDING ink color SWITCHING.*)

CYDNI
I legit got you into manga!

(*JANE closes the improvised painter's palette.*)

JANE
You took another STEM class—for fun! It's only fair.
Or should I say equivalent exchange?

(*CYDNI high-fives JANE. The static fades in on CAMERIN'S slight smile, The perspective returns to PAERCE. DAVIES brushes CAMERIN'S bracelets with*

relaxed fingers, while his wrist stiffens, as if the strands
will unweave without his effort.)

DAVIES
I'd buy these!

(CAMERIN looks down. ELLISON taps the paper
strands.)

ELLISON
You worked in a more delicate medium than me.
Dr. Rees—

(DAVIES cuts her off.)

ELLISON
Medaelia singled you out for good reason. She
wouldn't have done that if—

DAVIES
Don't hold back—she doesn't.

PAERCE (to himself)
Do it!

ELLISON
She'd tell you they were shit.

THESIS

(ELLISON uses the index and middle finger of one hand to touch the strands with finesse.)

ELLISON

What do these say?

(CAMERIN inhales.)

CAMERIN

Posts from active and inactive websites. In different languages—even conlangs.

PAERCE

Goddamn it, Cydni… .

(ELLISON and DAVIES admire the bracelets, angling the text so it catches the light. Meanwhile, CAMERIN and DAVIES eye ELLISON'S necklace. PAERCE sketches it on a blank page, rushing to label components. He restarts multiple times; the drawings improve over a handful of iterations. He labels the completed version "Discipline Sharing Workshop: Copper Wire, Ellison Jett".)

DAVIES

Why didn't you make the Iron Man suit!?

*(ELLISON laughs. CAMERIN glances at PAERCE, drawing

PAULINE UGALDE

the other's attention toward him too. They exchange waves, including PAERCE with his notepad.)

ELLISON

No—that's magic. I wanted something mundane.

(DAVIES nods, leans forward, pausing on the soldering where ELLISON recombined fragmented wires back together. PAERCE tracks DAVIES'S reactions and the wires' layout with his camera.)

ELLISON

I teach non-science majors to talk about science with people like them. I didn't want a scientific instrument—but I wanted working circuits.

(The guys laugh. ELLISON'S unphased. PAERCE smiles. He scribbles the phrase "hands-on projects > real-world examples" in his notes.)

PAERCE

I got B's in high school—you broke that trend.

(DAVIES relaxes. He hands off one vambrace to each tablemate.)

THESIS

DAVIES

Good—these were worth it.

(*CAMERIN and ELLISON laugh. CAMERIN squints at the musical notation and computer code on one vambrace. ELLISON hefts and flexes the other with both hands, pries at the glued, compressed paper layers with a fingernail. It holds.*)

CAMERIN

That text better not be the Necronomicon!

(*PAERCE laughs aloud before he can stifle himself. DAVIES gives him the thumbs-up.*)

DAVIES

No—that's Latin! This is Sclang—a programming language for musicians.

CAMERIN

But what's with the sheet music?

(*Alongside ELLISON, PAERCE compares the second vambrace to the first. Measures of music nested in paired brackets, parenthesis, and braces, mirror the vambrace with Sclang formatted like sheet music.*)

PAULINE UGALDE

ELLISON

Why's it formatted like Sclang?

DAVIES

Sclang makes music and coding accessible—for
musicians, and programmers.

SECURITY OFFICE, II

Muta jolts back. "But they didn't finish—" Their words rush out, imbued with Davies's residual enthusiasm and inflection.

Camerin nods but narrows his eyes at the change. "You've already observed the results."

He jerks his thumb out the door and down the hall. "This will overwhelm you."

Muta faces Camerin, seizing his hands before he can separate his bracelets again. "But Dana—"

Camerin shakes his head, pushes them off him, and curls their fingers around their improvised weapons. "She wanted you to tell everyone. But she wanted you to live."

He clamps his bracelet in one fist, straightens it, and poises its tip over his right eye. Muta's short boom pole clangs to the floor; they cradle the same location. Sharp head jerks emphasize their words: "I'm not a journalist. But she asked—demanded—I act like one. I can't flee from the truth."

One bracelet constricts Camerin's wrist, then the other. Muta's arms lower, their hands curl in their lap. "You're not running. You're protecting yourself."

Even while their disagreement carves onto their face, Muta mouths the words. "Your friends ran, they protected themselves."

They grimace against Camerin's unrelenting control, glaring at him. "This sacrifice isn't worth making."

Even while the rest of their body stiffens, Muta's tears fall unimpeded. "I can't look away. Why else would she risk her life to tell me?"

Camerin doesn't break eye contact, but his fingers twitch. "Paerce and Cydni escaped death. Like Kayleigh during the insurrection."

Camerin doesn't rebut. His shoulders slump, LIKE a weight lifted. "They saved me during COVID. I wasn't there—on January 6th, or last night. I have to be there now."

Camerin's bracelets unfurl once more. Muta's hands unclench. "Don't say I didn't warn you... ."

Muta sits up, pressing their hands together, as if praying. "Even if it hurts me? Show me the way."

9

CAFETERIA, II

MEDAELIA *climbs atop her table. Her and PAERCE stow their earbuds. Her headbanging slows, as she draws the symbols from her index card on the back of her hand. She raises her arms. Everyone quiets. CYDNI returns to her seat and nods in approval at PAERCE'S sketches. He points at the Supercollider vambrace.)*

PAERCE
"hypeassBass" isn't there. He loved that synth.
That can't be ours.

(CYDNI relaxes.)

CYDNI
Thank Arceus.

PAULINE UGALDE

(*MEDAELIA scans the crowd, calling out professors and journalists alike with her eyes.*)

MEDAELIA
Well? Show me.

(*JASON stands. PAERCE and CYDNI gape at a graphing calculator in his hands. Different fonts adorn the number pad, arithmetic functions, trigonometric functions, and menu buttons: Renaissance manuscripts, not modern fonts. As JASON moves, the screen ripples. Each button he touches pulsates like a heartbeat. Each data point he types with his index finger materializes in the same, pulsating font, until a set forms a tight spiral around him. CYDNI's eyes remain fixed on the display, in between covering and uncovering her face with her hands. PAERCE squints, his eyes tracing a path from JASON'S hands to the floating numbers for guiding wires that don't exist.*)

KAYLEIGH
Since when was he bending spoons?

JASON
I conducted multiple surveys. But I... extracted... nothing interesting.

THESIS

(MEDAELIA raises an eyebrow, climbs down, and stands next to him. PAERCE straightens, gawking at JASON.)

MEDAELIA
Elaborate.

JASON
Completing your objective seemed… impossible…
with a single object. Thus…

(He indicates his artifact. RENEE raises her hands: she wields an arm-length metal spring, a hook on one end and spike on the other. Approach, MEDAELIA inclines her head and grasps it in both hands, stretching then releasing it.)

RENEE
We interpreted your prompt differently.
You implied we should use qualitative factors
to inform our artifact—

(She points the spike downward.)

RENEE
I designed this with a local machine shop. Education
is a springboard for marginalized groups—some
truths must be told: However painful.

PAULINE UGALDE

MEDAELIA
And did you assist in its creation?

(RENEE beams, even before MEDAELIA finishes. JASON'S eye and hands twitch.)

CYDNI and **PAERCE** *(in unison, mouthed)*
Damn!

(KAYLEIGH whistles.)

RENEE
I used Midjourney. Made a mock up with
prompts within the shop's constraints.
And refined the prompt with their help.

JASON
If you want to embody your field, then why shackle
yourself to personal experiences?

(RENEE narrows her eyes and stands. MEDAELIA doesn't intervene.)

RENEE
You weren't even listening. This was
a creative exercise. People like you—

(JASON brandishes the calculator.)

THESIS

JASON

I extracted the essence of my work.

(His eyes turn white. With one hand, he enters data points. The X coordinate is 0, while Y rises at a constant rate. As each point appears around him, JASON raises his free hand from his side. RENEE levitates. She scrabbles for a handhold but can't pull herself back down. She grits her teeth, her soles graze the tabletop.)

RENEE

You didn't let me speak—and when you did? You didn't care.

(JASON holds her gaze. CYDNI indicates a projected graph above JASON'S head, which materialized once he entered three data points. The X-axis is labeled horizontal distance, and the Y-axis is labeled Altitude. MUTA'S professors, then their friends, share a long, hard glance.)

RENEE

You cared—when I was a test subject!

(She labors to lift her hands to shoulder height, fists throttling the spring. As she drags the spike across her

forearm, her eyes also turn white. Her palm grows transparent. The crowd gasps. PAERCE wretches and cover his mouth with his hands; his pen clatters to the floor. KAYLEIGH goes still and fixates on RENEE'S wound. JASON hesitates: For an instant, he levitates while mimicking her posture and expression, before thudding to the ground. He rounds the table, inching his arm forward as he closes the distance, eyes locked on RENEE. CYDNI smacks her phone onto her forehead mounting and sprints over to RENEE, tugging on her leg to no avail. PAERCE collapses CYDNI's phone stand and leaps over an occupied table to join his friend, yanking on RENEE'S other leg. CAMERIN clenches his hands, eyes wide as JASON halts RENEE inches from the ceiling. CAMERIN plunges one hand into his pocket.)

DAVIES

Are you gonna tell the cops
someone turned into Carrie!?

(CAMERIN sighs. JASON tilts his head away from his target's movements, as he creates a second line with an inverse slope to the first, intersecting once. She Strains against him, veins bulging in her forehead and shining with sweat. ELLISON jumps up and faces him, fists bawled at her sides. MUTA'S professors and friends gasp. Though she's within arm's reach of

THESIS

JASON, MEDAELIA is undeterred. She neither emotes nor moves.)

ELLISON

You've proven your point!

(Still tense, CYDNI and PAERCE step back. The man lowers his arm and his target.)

MEDAELIA

Agreed.

(MEDAELIA raises one hand. A blue-green arrow, with three branches diverging downward from a common stem, covers the back. PAERCE flashes the middle finger. CYDNI's nostrils flare. MEDAELIA slashes red ink across her throat and the arrows, and squeezes JASON'S shoulder. On contact, the tattoo's arrows point upward and outward toward RENEE. JASON veers his arm upward, his palms turning clear as His target hurtles past the students and into the far wall, behind MEDAELIA'S table. He pulls his arm back, bashing her into the wall again. Before he can do so a third time, RENEE lashes her spring into her hand, which whips through the air. JASON'S free hand slams into the tabletop over and over, bruising, gashes, spreading across his skin. With his other hand, he

accelerates manifesting numeric and graphical data, in concert with each strike. The X-axis is labeled Speed (meters/second), and the Y-axis is labeled Time (seconds).

She lets go of JASON. The professors' pupils dilate, their eyes change color, and fixate on him and RENEE. They square off against their colleagues—in shared and differing fields. Their artifacts and surrounding materials fuel their newfound powers. The first time each professor uses them, their palms turn clear. As one, CYDNI and PAERCE leap to their feet and mount their cameras on their shoulders. They sprint across and land ahead of a nearby table, ducking between combatants. They nod silently, facing the dividing wall. CYDNI follows PAERCE, who wall runs upward and rolls on his free shoulder on impact with the floor on the far side. Springing upright, they resume their escape, until a table blocks the isle. PAERCE scans the crowd.)

PAERCE
Too lethal.

(CYDNI nods. Two female professors, locked in combat, breach the crowd and emerge at the far end of the table. PAERCE zooms in on their silver eyes and transparent palms.)

CYDNI
Will you vouch for me in court?

(KAYLEIGH shares a dozen tabs of local and national news outlets and the Cupertino, California Police Department's contact pages.)

PAERCE
I can offer more than that.

KAYLEIGH
Finish them!

(CYDNI plants both hands on the table and vaults it, knees tucked to her chest. On landing, she hefts the nearest chair. Simultaneously, PAERCE drops into a roll underneath the table, emerging beside her only after CYDNI's armed. PAERCE unclips a pepper spray can from his belt and empties a payload into the obstructing professors' eyes. One lashes him with a scarf; the other widens metal restraints following an upside-down bell curve. A captive's wrists would be bound at the mean.

CYDNI shields PAERCE with her body and swings her chair into their ribs and groins. PAERCE stabs the distracted history professor through the ear, and the statistics professor at the base of the skull. CYDNI breaks the chair over their heads before leading him into the crowd.

Muta's professors circumvent the room, the two groups converging near the entrance. The majority of the closest, surrounding attendees target the professors; the rest attacking Muta's friends.

ELLISON steps in front of them, spreading her arms. PAERCE pepper sprays one man's eyes, and CYDNI raises her chair, but ELLISON gestures for her to stand down. Two wires detach from ELLISON, lashing PAERCE'S target's arms and chest, but he remains standing. The lights flicker, and ELLISON'S eyes flash white, with each blow. ELLISON loops together her thumbs and index fingers in front of her. The first wire binds his wrists to his sides, while the second shatters the nearest light fixtures and affixes to the exposed sockets. ELLISON punches toward him with both hands: Power surges through her circuit until he collapses.

The room goes dark. Behind her, DAVIES and CAMERIN link their arms, CAMERIN'S mouth and brows contorted in concentration. DAVIES splays CAMERIN'S fingers across his Supercollider code vambrace.)

THESIS

DAVIES (*shouting at him*)
I have a lead.

(*ELLISON nods at Muta's friends, who rearm themselves. She fences wire, sparking with electricity, around CAMERIN and DAVIES. DAVIES scribbles code on his arm. CAMERIN covers his eyes with his wrists. The nearest professors spasm, colliding full-speed with other combatants and blatant obstacles. ELLISON leads the way toward the exit.*)

PAERCE
ELLISON—take us to Muta.

(*ELLISON nods, unraveling and charging more wire. CYDNI shouts into her phone, PAERCE standing guard with a shard of metal in his free hand, cloth wrapping around the makeshift shiv's handle.*)

CYDNI (*to KAYLEIGH*)
Break the news!

(*KAYLEIGH can't hear CYDNI but nods anyway. Behind her, Patrick Schenk runs out KAYLEIGH'S bedroom door, the back of a bulletproof vest and handgun holster racing down the hall. As the footage ends, transcripts of concurrent phone calls with news stations near the Renewal University, and Lex Hoffman's driver's seat, flood her screen.)*

KAYLEIGH
Lex! There's a terror attack at RE!
Patrick—get 911—and the news! Stay with me!

'10

SECURITY OFFICE, III

However long Camerin and Muta have known each other, Muta's reactions surprise him. As he expected, Cydni and Paerce, alive and well, renew their morale. They laugh at their friends' jokes and copy their mannerisms on reflex. Camerin can't hold back his joy when they clasp their hands and intone "Worship," as Paerce vibes to his music to lift his spirits. Their eyes trace an identical path through the crowd, optimizing interviews conducted and distance traveled.

In an instant, they flush with anger. Their outraged sobs synchronize with Jason telekinetically controlling Renee. When he controls his enemy, over the rising psychic static, they ask, "When did you go bad?"

They wince, emulating Renee's pain. Sickened

yet engrossed by Camerin's visions, like a virtual reality game, they puppet Jason's movements and blank expression. Muta raises their hands and rakes their fingernails across their forearm, when Renee weaponizes her defiance. From behind them, Camerin shudders, as four years of anger, fear, and loneliness slam into him, emotions that Muta's friends failed to quell.

Muta's hazel eyes go wide, and they hyperventilate, as Renee dents the wall. Camerin covers his face. A memory loops in his mind: A police officer's head slammed into a door by a riot shield over, and over, and over, wielded by a man in tactical gear. A mob's cries of fabricated grievance drown out the victim's screams.

Lying on his back, his body stiff and drenched with sweat, Camerin sits up, grappling with a weight on his chest. He hides none of his pain, surprise over the transmission, or desire to downplay both, however intense. "Come on, don't take this out on me."

Muta's shoulders tense. Camerin sighs. His naked turmoil foils his efforts to project calm. "Cydni taught me a trick for this. Stay with me here."

Silent recognition dons on Muta's face; their panic remains. "Close your eyes," he instructs. He stays unmoving until Muta obeys.

His eyes shine. "Picture a feather floating in front of you."

A golden feather, plucked from Camerin's mind's eye, so real he could reach out and touch it, hovers between them. Muta's eyes flutter open, and one hand combs through the air over the feather, before dropping back down.

"See it?"

They nod, still shaking.

"Your breathing keeps that feather floating—"

Camerin fights the tension in Muta's body: They don't proceed without him. "Just breathe slow and steady, in and out."

Camerin demonstrates; the ethereal feather rising and falling in time with his and Muta's lockstep breathing; they didn't need him to elaborate on the exercise. The turbulence in the feather's rhythm smooths out.

Muta opens their eyes and lies back. Camerin cushions their head with his jacket. He resumes the video feed of the walkway outside with a tilt of his head. He checks the barricade again and sits across the room, waiting until his friend falls asleep. Eyes glowing a faint silver and locked on the door, hands folded in his lap, Camerin unbuckles the camera. Without its display facing him, he reads its battery indicator, and the video's size. It grows another megabyte beyond the SD card's capacity in real time. *I can point at every muscle they tensed when Renee died—but I assumed I didn't need the feather... .*

Slumping, he telekinetically films himself. "I made it, Dana."

He checks the clock: it's half past five. He sighs. *How long was Emery awake?*

"I'll update the record with what I know till Muta wakes up. I hope they don't mind... ."

Dimming the lights, he whispers to them, "Time to follow Dana and Daniel's lead."

(CAMERIN inclines his head toward the desk. The laptop floats toward him. He converses with his colleagues, mouthing his responses. The back of his head vibrates with bone conduction. Whenever someone speaks, he turns toward an invisible person whispering in his ear from behind.)

ELLISON

They won't like you snooping—no
matter the reason you're doing it.

(Radio static crackles in her voice. CAMERIN runs the bare wire in one bracelet between his fingers; the crackle fades.)

THESIS

CAMERIN

They couldn't stop talking about this—before
and after they came back to school.

*(Muta's laptop opens. The touchpad cursor stumbles
across their desktop.)*

CAMERIN

Even if they sent me images at three A.M.
that totally aren't serial killer trophies... .

*(His friends laugh. DAVIES shrugs—or rather, CAMERIN
copies him. He fumbles with the controls until he places
the shaded rectangle from the 'options' portion of the
menu, into a central, empty rectangle. He opens and
confirms the 'Delete save data' prompt. In the main
menu, the glitchy effect persists on the 'New game'
option. CAMERIN'S hand scrolls the game cursor to
'Options' again, but he jerks it back to 'Continue'; his
eyes didn't stray from the 'New Game'.)*

CAMERIN

DAVIES. Deleting the save data doesn't fix that.

*(DAVIES' raised eyebrow Superimposes over
CAMERIN'S vision.)*

PAULINE UGALDE

DAVIES

If anyone could edit game data in real time? It's you.

(CAMERIN *laughs. He glances over at* MUTA, *fast asleep.*)

CAMERIN

Right back at you. But why bother? How
does the game put it? "Victory doesn't
mean anything if you don't earn it?"

(DAVIES *nods. He leans forward, quivering, swirling blackness emerging onto the outermost layer of his vambraces.*)

DAVIES

I don't wanna slow you down but, could I help?

(CAMERIN *almost drops the controller.* DAVIES *stands and spins around, his silver eyes fixed on the wall behind him. Duct tape sutures together butcher paper enveloping his walls. The sheets burst with shifting code, film screenshots, graphs of statistical models, and human biological diagrams.* DAVIES *and* ELLISON'S *research even adorns the windows and the back of the only door.*

THESIS

ELLISON sits facing it, braiding a tangle of wires together. CAMERIN sits, steadying one hand on the desk.)

CAMERIN
Are you safe?

(ELLISON nods on DAVIES' behalf: he vibes to the menu music, a minimalistic, chiptune beat. Even as CAMERIN looks away from his screen and toward the wall adjacent to MUTA, DAVIES' office overlays CAMERIN'S line of sight.)

CAMERIN
Actually? Can you replace the music with
what The Discyples—made?

(DAVIES cuts his reply short, straightening and looking where CAMERIN would sit in person.)

DAVIES
How long will this take?

(CAMERIN stills. He averts his gaze. DAVIES holds firm.)

DAVIES
You can't hide anymore… .

PAULINE UGALDE

(CAMERIN'S eyes well with tears. He shakes his head.)

CAMERIN
I... I'm still not ready. I don't deserve you.
After what I did.

(He doesn't stop, as he clicks 'continue'. The game opens on a black screen, unbroken except for piercing through him. ELLISON and DAVIES look at each other. She wraps one of her wires around DAVIES'S wrist but releases him. As she does, he sighs and nods at her. They both focus on CAMERIN, as he scrolls through the opening text, delivered by an unseen speaker. A bass tone reverberates throughout each line.)

Steeling himself, Camerin rolls up one sleeve. A glowing scar, switching between vibrant blues and greens, emerges, its arrows branching forward and outward, connected by a common stem. The wires in his bracelets overlay the shape, and he traces it with a finger. Ellison's and Davies's faces fade from Camerin's mind; their presences, conversation, and actions, filter, like enabling noise cancelation. He compartments their telepathic link.

(PAERCE falling backward, CYDNI rushing to his side, and seizing his head in her hands before he slams into

the tile, fills CAMERIN'S vision. Clenching his hands into fists, CAMERIN faces MUTA. PAERCE looks behind him and gropes for the back of his head, but CYDNI holds him firm. He shakes his head at where CAMERIN would be in person. CAMERIN nods. On his back, PAERCE grips CYDNI'S shoulders, with sudden strength. Her eyes widen. She touches the parts of her skull that PAERCE pointed out. CAMERIN grimaces and pushes into his seat with his full weight, as if fighting to sit upright against PAERCE atop him, while maintaining eye contact with MUTA.)

CAMERIN

They're coming back for you.

(Muted, CYDNI and PAERCE speak rapid fire to each other. Their movements buffer or jerk, a livestream with spotty Internet. CYDNI places PAERCE'S laptop on the ground. He types 'Thank you' in one tab before switching to an active Discord video call. KAYLEIGH leans forward, brown eyes intent on his face. CYDNI redirects her to focus behind PAERCE'S shoulder. She complies. In the Discord chat, a message from Pluribus appears: "Romero's not there." PAERCE unfolds his shirt collar, revealing a wire necklace, the woven, trifurcated symbol resting over his heart. He presses one hand over both. KAYLEIGH shares her laptop

PAULINE UGALDE

screen, standing and rotating around her room. Extra monitors display local and national news broadcasts. Anchors, still and silent, take frantic, drawn and transcribed notes.)

PAERCE
Thanks. For the feather.

(CAMERIN nods, his posture wavering while he homes in on the spot at PAERCE'S eye level. CYDNI unveils the same trifurcated wire design on a bracelet on her left wrist, holding it to the inside edge with her thumb. CAMERIN cuts her off—he can't hear her whatsoever. CYDNI'S features contort in concentration, before she lunges toward PAERCE'S desk. She plugs earbuds into one branch of a USB splitter: a dongle with three earphone jacks. In the middle one, she inserts the trifurcated arrows originating branch. The apparatus flush with her wrist, PAERCE and KAYLEIGH, the rest of the group MUTA calls The Discyples, follow. CAMERIN'S telepathic buffering ceases.)

THE DISCYPLES (in unison)
We're the writing on the wall, the whispers in the classroom. But without Emery? We are nothing.

(KAYLEIGH's voice crackles with radio static.)

THESIS

KAYLEIGH

Me and Emery said the same thing to death.

(KAYLEIGH produces her own stripped wire and earphone splitter. While wearing the earphones in one jack, she copies CYDNI'S trifurcated arrow placement, before speaking into it like a lapel mic.)

KAYLEIGH

Not today.

(CAMERIN smiles. Extending his right thumb and index finger, curling all other fingers inward, a hook remains.)

CYDNI

Thanks for finding Muta for us, Professor—

(CAMERIN shakes his head.)

CAMERIN

Camerin.

(CYDNI and PAERCE mime firing shotguns at the backs of their heads, grinning. A wavering image of CAMERIN in his seat, silver eyes and mock shotgun and all, appears behind PAERCE'S shoulder. CYDNI follows

PAULINE UGALDE

PAERCE'S gaze toward CAMERIN, after a delay and offset by a foot. KAYLEIGH shrugs, but she performs the shooting gesture last. CAMERIN looks away from MUTA and relaxes. The vision vanishes. He pulls up his sleeve and brushes his fingers against his wires. DAVIES and ELLISON'S voices and senses overtake him again.)

11

EXTERIOR, ADMISSIONS BUILDING, I

Muta wakes, flailing, and falls; Camerin catches their shoulders, before balancing Muta's water bottle on their chest. His index finger and thumb gingerly handle the neck, as if it will shatter if he squeezes it any tighter.

Camerin finishes one of their stolen drinks, Muta chugging the water bottle. "Hey, you. You're finally awake!"

Muta spit takes. "We're not driving a carriage! I'm not handcuffed! Why?"

Camerin grins. "Should I have said that I want to play a game?

"Or that you aren't the first person to lose an eye here?"

Muta snickers and sits up, spotting their open, humming laptop on the desk beside Camerin. He looks away, but not before giving his friend a sheepish smile. Muta intercepts Camerin's incoming embarrassment: "I would've let you try the first..."

Instead of glowing eyes, fixed on a hewn wooden table, pixilated art fills the screen. As he ends his session, a green, not brown tint, colors the main menu. They flip the screen down. "Did you mark your ambition?"

Camerin's smile broadens. He mimics Muta's fist bump but withdraws his hands into his lap. "I saw where most of your cut thesis material came from."

Muta raises their eyebrows. Camerin continues, "You're not giving the second act enough credit. After all, if it wasn't there, the rest wouldn't hit as hard."

They sigh. Muta humors him, even as their jaw sets, and they arm themselves with their arguments. "The mystery's interesting. But adjusting to all the new things sucked. All the new people and mechanics... ."

Camerin counters, "But the acting sold it. Realistic cringe. Great period piece."

"The actor reminded me of you."

Camerin takes Muta's shoulder and squeezes it, before they can overanalyze him. "Sincere and cringe."

Muta's eyes prickle, but he preempts their

tears: "Some people objected, but on my playthrough, I chose Technology. Of course."

Muta smiles in return, stows their computer, and checks the time. They fling their bag on their shoulders. "Crap!"

Camerin interrupts with a hand on Muta's forearm: "Yes—I let you sleep."

He pauses for an instant, tapping into the stimuli transferring between them through one of his bracelets, almost cutting through their T-shirt to bear down on their skin. Their stream of questions arrives in his mind's eye like shotgun shells penetrating his skull, vivid and frantic. The pair flinch together, as Camerin's eyes flash silver while he parses each question silently. "The building's secure. I'm unhurt. I tapped out after finishing the second act. Yes—I slept. But nobody came." He indicates the diligent, floating camera. "No—I don't know how the battery is still working." Camerin turns toward the door. "And the others will be here soon."

Muta doesn't wait for Camerin to finish. "Any word about the party?"

Camerin shakes his head. Their touch floods the most lurid sensations from the video—memory— back into both of them. Though Muta sets their jaw and stays silent, Camerin responds aloud, as if Muta voiced their turmoil. "I'm sorry. I didn't—couldn't—

filter out excess stimuli. I should've disconnected but I couldn't look away."

Muta's shoulders sink. Camerin concludes, even while their shared dismay hangs between them. "But, no. Nothing's changed."

Muta looks up from their packed bag. "Did you help me stay asleep?"

They mount the camera on their shoulder and stand, Camerin leading the way into the hall. He doesn't hide his surprise. "It's just brainwave manipulation—electromagnetic radiation. And you were already highly suggestable, after the... After the feather mini game."

Muta walks in Camerin's footsteps, but their eyes look far off. He can almost read the analysis etched on their face. "I know what sleep is. You were a strong empath—No. You were a strong scanner."

Camerin shrugs and responds with a smile of recognition. "But I still don't understand my..."

The camera embodies his nuanced, yet continuous thoughts, like a human cocking their head or steepling their fingers. "Powers... ."

Muta peers into the lobby and offers Camerin their long boom pole, one hand leading the other along its length. Camerin studies their grip, feeling out its weight with his own uncertain swings. "Don't worry. Even I know you're not an X-Man."

Muta puts on their best Deadpool impression: "Since you're tough, morally flexible, and young enough so you can carry a franchise ten to twelve years."

Camerin guffaws. "Like the X Force—"

The lights sputter out.

Muta grabs the soft drink closest to the top of their backpack, poised to hurl it outside. Camerin steps in front of them without hesitation, wielding the boom pole like a staff. He leads them into the afternoon sunshine and shushes them with his free hand. Unprompted, his bracelets crackle, and the camera detaches from Muta's shoulder and floats away. On the facing side of the wall Muta scaled, metal glints, and a woman greets: "Hey, you. You're finally awake!"

As Ellison approaches, two wires loosen from around her neck. One caresses and wraps around the camera to face her, even while her hands tense at her sides. The other draws a rippling line connecting her and Camerin's silver eyes. Muta's eardrums pop.

Camerin pantomimes offense. "Hey—don't steal my joke!"

Ellison squeezes his arm. Camerin flinches. "I didn't steal it. You let me hear it."

Wedge shaped outlines flash across their vision, surrounding the group, and a third man—

Davies leaves cover, hands clasped: He's tired and unkempt, but unhurt. Muta embraces him. The wedges partition the group off from their surroundings. "We're good," he reassures, as his eyes flare from brown to white.

He points to the pavement, paired, ethereal brackets enclose everyone, demarking the matching, wedged walls. Before the left bracket, is the abbreviation 'amp', and a zero is written to the right of the right one. "No one can hear us. It's anechoic and soundproof."

Ellison nods in approval. Muta squints at his vambraces. Unlike the writing in their friends' footage, Davies' code flows and drips down his forearm. Davies caves in under their scrutiny. "I learned to project my thoughts from Ellison."

His words appear on one vambrace, proceeded by two slashes: How Supercollider denotes a programmer's comments. Camerin nods. "Dana did the same for her artifact—but not for music and physics. For film and game design."

(As Davies narrates, a conversation from The Discyples' server projects on the inside of Muta's eyelids. An exchange between her and Muta crawls down their field of vision, almost too fast to read.)

THESIS

Category: Fandom
#inscryption, (text channel)
No blood required.

Selfsacrificed · 5/17/24, at 6:05 PM
@Mutavault I didn't think you'd be down for a nothing is scarier vibes! But Mullins pulls it off!

Mutavault · 5/17/24, at 6:05 PM
@Selfsacrificed Duh. It's just eyes! At least Bily the puppet gave you a face!

(Screenshots with blurred edges and objects of interest distorted, as if traced and drawn in haste, separate each pair of messages.)

Selfsacrificed · 5/17/24, at 6:05 PM
@Mutavault The boss fight monologues are so detailed. Sensory.

Mutavault · 5/17/24, at 6:05 PM
@selfsacrificed And disgusting. 😣😣😣😣😣😣

(As Dana posts, colored highlights pepper the dialogue in the same screenshots. Dana's versions have unbroken edges and undistorted visuals.)

PAULINE UGALDE

Category: School
#help, (text channel)
When gen AI, Google, and YouTube tutorials suck.

Selfsacrificed · 5/17/24, at 6:06 PM
@Mutavault Do you think the dialogue from Act I could help my lower division students?

Mutavault · 5/17/24, at 6:06 PM
😔😔😔??

(The highlights superimpose over Muta's vision, outlining Muta's comments and each server member as they join the conversation. Technicolor arrows link reply threads. Blue and green highlights trace Daniel's posts, also written on May 17.)

PhaseChanger · 5/17/24, at 6:06 PM
@Mutavault Damn! Emery is this where your tattoo is from!?

Mutavault · 5/17/24, at 6:06 PM
@PhaseChanger Fuck yeah it is!

PhaseChanger · 5/17/24, at 6:06 PM
@Selfsacrificed Dana your hype did it for me. I know what I'm doing for my artifact.

THESIS

(Selfsacrificed reacted with 😁)
(Mutavault reacted with 📸)

PhaseChanger · Today at 6:07 PM
2 days of procrastination are over!

(The crawl ends on a post from Dana at 6:07 PM, in the Gaming Spoilers text channel, in the Spoilers category. She attached an edited screenshot, of a rainbow colored card, extra rainbow effects layered atop it, tagging Muta, Cydni, and Paerce. Muta's skull hums with their memory of her voice.)

DANA (*voiceover*)
No wonder you can't shut up about this!
New game here I come!

Muta freezes, as their head tilts to read the screenshots, like an intangible VR screen over their face. Once they reach Daniel's post, their eyes water, before they begin crying, their body wracked by quiet, yet intense sobs that threaten to unbalance them.

Davies halts. Ellison jabs him in the ribs with her elbow. He winces at each blow, sparks crackling between them. He face-palms, a multitude of swears forming on his lips. They don't manifest as words, but as a torrent of unfiltered thoughts: Directed at himself, not his friends.

In their own ways, everyone reflects his inner conflict over how to respond and tortured expressions. Ellison's arm drops to her side, and Camerin wipes tears from her cheeks. At last, Davies settles on: "We had multiple chances to learn this—"

A voice cuts Davies off. Muta stops crying and looks up, but Davies takes Muta's chin and directs them to behold his vambraces instead. They vibrate alongside Paerce's voice. "If only I had possessed the humility to say to myself, 'I have seen enough for one life.'"

Muta shudders with recognition. The frames of Dana's film roll wiz past in front of them, stopping on a loop of the two corpses shielding each other. Davies lets go. He addresses a spot above Muta's head. "You didn't have to do that. They know we failed every time."

As a sad laugh slips out, and Paerce continues: "'I have done my part.'"

Davies nods. The other professors following. Captivated by the vambraces' surfaces, Muta nods last. Davies' affirmation scrolls across the paper and rings in Muta's mind.

We won't split the party again.

He hesitates. Ellison and Camerin flash him looks. Camerin taps his bracelets, and Davies... nods? Did he respond, or did he psyche himself up? He steadies himself, amending: *No matter what sacrifices must be made.*

Muta yelps and spasms, their prior caution evaporating. "How do you know—!?"

Davies cackles, Paerce and—

Paerce and CYDNI follow suit. He leads the group, the brackets following them, away from the admissions building. "I heard the original version of the song The Discyples covered for the midterm. While Camerin was playing."

While holding up air quotes to either side of his head: "That 'hypeass chiptune trap metal boss theme' you pulled an all-nighter for?"

Muta spasms again but can't resist headbanging to imaginary music. Several seconds behind the others , they hurry to catch up. Over their footsteps, Paerce's sincerity bypasses space and time. "'Then again, there is no greater glory than fighting to find the truth.'"

Muta turns to one side and smiles in agreement, shaking the same illusory numbers from their vision as the ones they saw on the route to the building. The numbers swarm them, sharpening the faster they blink. The illusion of—

Camerin's in front of them, poised to take their shoulders. Muta lets him. Camerin clears imaginary debris out of his eyes: "I was afraid you'd see that. It gives us one more reason to leave."

He gestures for Muta to follow. "We'll carjack something from the   philosophy building's parking lot."

Emphatically: "Together."

Ellison slows to Muta's pace, arcing the camera around toward her. "We failed the first time."

Muta raises their voice. Everyone startles. "Ellison—you killed someone. The press can say whatever they want without getting sued. They'd pay a billion dollars to slander you. What were you gonna do when you left?"

Everyone groans, even while covering their mouths or turning away. "Fuck the police! They treat normal people like shit—what will they do to us—to me? Where will we go !?"

In the instant before Davies speaks, Camerin and Ellison—and the other Discyples—laugh: "Not Florida."

Muta's humor and cringe almost topples them.

Suddenly, a sharp, echoing bang. Two of Ellison's wires tighten around Muta's wrists and tug them behind a pile of rubble. A man sprints by: One hand over his head, the other grasping at his neck, eyes scrutinizing his surroundings. As he passes, the bang rings out again. Muta flinches, readying for a spray of bullets.

None comes.

Ellison, Davies, and Camerin trade a glance, before Camerin clamps his hands over Muta's mouth, pinning one of their arms. Ellison unreels wires from her belt and jeans' pockets, weaving them together with swift, silent, minute hand movements. Even her twitching, silver eyes shape the metal. As Muta watches, Ellison retrieves their pocket knife from their belt and cuts away excess fabric and cables from their camera rig. When she's done, she's woven a head mounting for their camera. Davies's Supercollider code flickers across the fabric. Muta doesn't understand most of it, except for kg, the metric abbreviation for mass, and 9.8 m/s, The acceleration of gravity on a freefalling object. As they read it, the same code projects around their harness.

As she works, she glares daggers toward the confrontation beyond the rubble.

Even as they turn their head in confusion, they tug at the camera, mounted on their forehead. Friction from the reappropriated straps leading out of it rubs against their touch, but the camera glides, weightless. As they crane their neck toward the panicking man, Camerin's hands still clamped over their mouth, the camera, head mount, and their rig's weight, doesn't burden them at all.

'12

EXTERIOR, MACREADY BUILDING PARKING LOT, II

DR. JOSH MEYERS, *in his late 30s and bloodied casual clothes, stands shaking, hands raised in surrender. JANE, blood spattering her jeans and T-shirt, blocks the shortest path out of campus.)*

JOSH

S-s-stop!

(He offers his wallet, splayed open. The woman claps, overlapping pairs of pentagons on the backs of her hands, and the preexisting, interlocking, triangular symbols on her arms, glow. White light flashes within the holes in her palms. The concrete underneath him erupts upward, dragging him down. Wrists pinned

under him, he sprawls. ELLISON'S hands shake. DAVIES leans in.)

DAVIES
Where's her artifact?

(JANE approaches JOSH at a slow walk. Straining against the weight bearing down on him, he sits up, but she seizes him by the hair with one hand. With the other, she snaps her fingers. His sleeve ignites. He screams, poised to smother it with sand scraped off the ground. She snaps again: It extinguishes. The prone man quakes in her grip.)

ELLISON
Her.

(DAVIES squints at JANE. Code fragments flicker on his vambraces, synchronized with his quickening breath, audible through his hands pressed over his face. JANE extracts concrete and dirt out from between her feet and encases her clenched fist; wrist; and forearm. She punches the floor next to JOSH'S torso.)

DAVIES
What's her ignition source?

THESIS

MUTA
Ambient oxygen—

(ELLISON shakes her head. Her wires snap at the air.)

ELLISON
The snap ignites it. It's impossible to create
something out of nothing.

(CAMERIN inches toward his allies, gasping. ELLISON clamps her hands over his mouth. CYDNI'S voice whispers at ELLISON'S side. MUTA and CAMERIN mouth along with her.)

CYDNI *(voiceover)*
Something of equal value must be given.

(DAVIES nods to himself. ELLISON taps the back of MUTA'S head with a wire. Eyes locked on theirs, ELLISON releases CAMERIN and slashes a finger twice across her throat. The visions of CYDNI and PAERCE'S mangled corpses flash across the inside of MUTA'S eyelids. In the last vision, the crouched JOSH'S silver eyes peer out from behind MUTA'S friends: one hand throttling his neck chain, the other covering his mouth.)

PAULINE UGALDE

JOSH

I'll w-w-wire you my savings. M-m-my SSN is Six-six-six—

(JANE doesn't move.)

JOSH

I'll never teach again! I'll change my n-n-name! I'll leave th-th-the country!

(JOSH'S eyes widen, pleading. JANE stares through him and claps. He tackles her, poised to headbutt her. DAVIES stifles a whistle. Metal scraping beneath the ground, a spear as thick as JANE'S wrist and as long as her thigh emerges between the pair. Still filming, MUTA shoves CAMERIN off of them and wall runs up the rubble pile, before their body shifts into a wall bounce and corner boost. As they execute a one-handed vault, they lob their soda can at JANE'S head. She claps. It fragments. The largest, most jagged pieces angle outward and orbit her. Rolling on impact on their unburdened shoulder, MUTA rises, the rest of JANE'S spear levitating from the ground, its tip pointing at their chest. MUTA unfolds their pocket knife, capping their closed fist with their thumb: an edge-outward, reverse grip. As the spear flies toward them, they block it with the boom pole, their stance holding even as the boom pole fractures. They flank JANE and jab her in the stomach with the pole's jagged end. The spear ricochets toward JANE, who ducks and stabs toward MUTA'S ribs. The top layer of overlapping notepads in Daniel's vest stops the spear tip from penetrating further. MUTA stabs into the holes in her hands and kicks her in the groin.

ELLISON repels down from the top of the rubble pile; wires anchored into it dictate her trajectory and slow her fall. She lands upright next to MUTA. Electricity jumps from her fingertips to the still moving spear. Looping her index fingers and thumbs together, she entraps JANE'S arms at her sides. Stray debris strikes JOSH, but his eyes flash white. His concrete handcuffs and neck chain crumble. The debris slams into his chest but doesn't cut him or his clothing. ELLISON reels in the other half of MUTA'S boom pole and mirrors their grip, her wires deflecting the same debris that almost shredded JOSH. JANE'S eyes and palms revert. She relaxes.)

JANE
Is Dr. Meyers—Josh—dead?

(ELLISON laughs shortly and stands her ground. CAMERIN gestures for DAVIES to circumvent the rubble. DAVIES codes The noise canceling bubble around them.)

ELLISON
This time? No.

(CAMERIN reaches the sitting JOSH first, kneeling next to him as JOSH stretches his bare, lacerated feet out. JANE averts her gaze. DAVIES rushes out, banishing the silencer.)

JANE
Finish me off, then. Or should I?

(ELLISON scans the symbols on JANE'S hands: They're drawn in blood, not ink. ELLISON'S shoulders quake.)

ELLISON
The Discyples would kill me if I did.

(JANE shakes her head.)

JANE (to herself)
It felt like days I was chasing him. I kidnapped him—garroted him.

(MUTA shushes her.)

THESIS

MUTA
ELLISON's right: while we're here, you won't hurt him.

(MUTA'S eyes trace her symbols.)

ELLISON
Too late.

(Looking up at CAMERIN, binding JOSH'S feet with Sclang-covered strips from his jacket, JANE laughs. JOSH joins her, shoulders sagging. CAMERIN'S eyes flare silver; MUTA'S surroundings vanish, superseded by CYDNI and PAERCE, backs pressed against a wall. CAMERIN stands in front of both, shielding them from an approaching, white-eyed crowd. Stiffening his posture, CAMERIN encircles his ribcage with, and tugs on, his bracelets six times, jerking his own body back each time. The six closest people keel over, kicking, clawing, biting, whoever they touch. Inert defenders' ribcages cave under their attackers' weight. Blood cascades through the crowd's palm holes onto the asphalt.

A seventh professor, dripping with blood from killing the attackers below her on the pile, stands. CAMERIN flings himself backward and stabs the tips of his bracelets, now straightened, into his palms, spreading his arms to further shield CYDNI and PAERCE. The professor, likewise, falls on her back, the bones in her hands crunching as CAMERIN'S mock knives pin her outspread arms down. Rising, CAMERIN reconnects his bracelets and tightens them above his ears, the ends crossed over his forehead. Flushing with rage, knuckles bleached white, he flings the bracelets up and away from his head. A shotgun blast rings in MUTA'S ears, as the seventh professor's head explodes. Even after the vision dissipates, CAMERIN'S eyes don't revert, and MUTA gapes at him. DAVIES stands beside him.)

JANE (to ELLISON)
Fair. But I shouldn't burden you with killing again.

(DAVIES quivers, until his eyes match CAMERIN'S, and his vambraces burst with code. Variables at the top include the number of stairs to his office and height off the ground floor. Underneath, bracketed arrays record accelerating stair numbers and heights, until the stair number peaks, and the height plummets to zero. The name of the variable affected by plummeting downstairs changes from tBD, to millerReck. MUTA falls sidelong, dropping the camera, hands clamped on their face. ELLISON catches them by hand and with a woven, wire net. CAMERIN reaches for DAVIES, who recoils: He's about to cry. Both men's eyes revert. JANE nods to herself and seizes the camera. ELLISON whips a wire out from her belt, but retracts it as JANE tilts the camera, capturing her tattoos and gore-smeared clothes. MUTA'S eyes fly open.)

JANE
Tell. Everyone.

(She claps. The spear transmutes into twin daggers with brass knuckles and sharpened spurs on the pommels, plus matching sheaths, bearing blood-red pentagons. One dagger clenched in their fist, MUTA hacks at their dyed red hair, until it brushes their chin. They clip the sheaths to their belt.)

JANE (to ELLISON)
Have I done enough for you?

(ELLISON nods, gritting her teeth. She points her taut wires at JANE, who stands. Under ELLISON'S gaze, JANE hurries away in the direction where MUTA came from. JOSH stands, retrieving MUTA'S short boom pole from the ground. His neck chain reforms, each link comprised of a unique material and shape.)

JOSH
Camerin? Tell the other Discyples—

(CYDNI'S voice cuts JOSH off. Muta's professors' artifacts reverberate.)

CYDNI (voiceover)
What do we say to death?

(Draping one arm over JOSH'S shoulder, CAMERIN wraps him in an embrace with the other. JOSH reciprocates and limps away.)

JOSH (over his shoulder)
Not today.

'13

EXTERIOR, MACREADY BUILDING
PARKING LOT, III

Ellison unspools unbloodied wires, her arms outspread, her colleagues shielded by her body. *Get them in the shot—and fix Daniel's vest first.*

The command compels Muta's fingers to sacrifice the duct tape strips hugging their jacket close, which promote parkour aerodynamics.

Camerin creates his rope and hands one end off to Davies. His fists clenched at his chest, knuckles touching, and eyes pinpointed on Camerin, code pours onto Davies' vambraces. The anechoic bubble swallows them, the interior brightens and darkens, the shadows dull and cut deeper. Even the temperature of the air and concrete change with apparent light exposure. Patching Daniel's vest without looking down, Muta keeps a vigilant eye on the screen. Their phone's battery level history reads, *'Battery level ranged between seventy and seventy-five percent between twelve P.M. and eight P.M.'* When Davies stops, the time stills to eight P.M.

The sun accelerates toward the horizon. The outdoor lights flicker on, wavering over the darkening campus.

Ellison smiles weakly. "Where do you think I've been getting my electricity from?"

Muta gives a thumbs up. Davies draws the party's attention. Variables above his vambraces' code, shorthand for different times, environmental conditions, and group permutations, occupy one block. "We'll have a common frame of reference," Davies reassures Muta. "And our powers will work even after we leave."

Davies points to his bare arms, alight with code. "Like Jane. And your party's tattoos. We have these?"

He points out identical code on Camerin and Ellison, with his finger and the zoomed camera lens. "So we can use our powers."

Ellison asks, as Davies leads the way toward the deserted parking lot, "Cops will want us to erase it—when they arrest us—like disarming ourselves."

Davies's chuckle grates against his friends'

eardrums—and the insides of their skulls. No one flinches or cuts him off. *They'd have to flay us.*

Camerin walks to his side, his own sad laugh slipping out. He gazes toward the surrounding streets. "Not like they could stop us from recreating them. But I'm keeping mine. For my lawyer."

Muta copies his laugh. "Amen. Dana spent her last moments doing the *Blair Witch* apology. Breaking the law—jail—can't be worse—"

They squint at Davies's code. On the first line, static covers the word 'New', then clears. The word 'Continue' replaces 'New'. Davies swipes the text like a smartphone screen. "Good catch. It's factoring in our location. So our powers will work off campus—"

Muta points, insisting. 'Continue' replaces the same instance of the word 'New', and static obscures the whole line, as Muta's skull resonates with a short, harsh drone. *Is my lack of sleep catching up with me again?*

Davies slows his pace, the camera, guided by his technopathy, tracking his slowed, yet fluid movements. "This is the most complex thing the three of us have done with our powers. We're literally rewriting the laws of nature—"

The rising drone drowns him out. 'New' switches to 'Continue' again. Muta stabilizes the camera with both hands, zooming in on the text.

The glitching and droning repeat. Deep, quiet, yet discordant tones catch their attention. They cock their head, discerning an electronic, closed high hat, and matching drum kick layered on top, the instruments' tempo and rhythm mimicking a heartbeat. Their eyes widen. Camerin nods. "Davies—our code's making sound."

Muta shakes, their clammy, clumsy hands refusing to peel their professors' hands off the rope. They lock their eyes on Camerin. "I heard this when I woke up earlier. The menu opened itself. And glitched."

Davies stops to listen, springing to action after one note. Unsheathing one of Muta's daggers, he flays the vambraces' topmost layer, backpedaling as Ellison's wires shred it. He and Camerin renew the grip on the rope with both hands, their code fighting to function, to tread water amid the intruding tide.

As Muta feared, 'Continue' replaces 'New' again, written in glitching, rotating, three-dimensional letters which float out and in front of the surface. The letters take the rest of the code block hostage.

A chiptune bang grates, hammers a gavel on a table. Their unlocked, floating phone reads, ten-thirty P.M. Their surroundings, the remaining lit screen, and their professors' silver eyes, fade to black.

'14

CAFETERIA, III

Muta wakes.

Another student?

A whisper reverberates in their skull and bones. The darkness envelopes their hand in front of their face. Muta can't lift their hands. They're bound, but they can move. Ellison's necklace glints in front of their hands, but doesn't touch, let alone handcuff them. They muster the breath and will to speak, but—

The gray eyes staring back at them transfix their words on their tongue.

It has been ages.

Medaelia stands. Her black jeans, matching hoodie, framing her face, and tinted, matching sunglasses, enhance the illusion of disembodied eyes.

They almost glow from behind the lenses. Even after Muta blinks several times, it remains—hell, it *intensifies* as they watch.

Muta laughs from shock, their head peeking out over their floating camera, separating the two of them. Its languid rotations bear witness to both their and Medaelia's reactions.

Medaelia drums her fingers on the table. Posture straight yet relaxed, she drinks Muta in. The next time she looks away, Muta finds their professors, sitting at a table behind them, Muta's open, activated laptop in front of them. With great effort, they conceal their relieved sigh. Ellison's wires branch across the keyboard, diverging into five segments, splayed at equal intervals. Two short, woven segments form crosshairs, at the base of the rightmost wire.

They clasp their hands. From behind them, a chair shifts, but Medaelia meets their gaze again, burning with curiosity, before they can find the source. She tilts her head.

They accept her offer, scanning their captor? Like the Discyples' footage, glowing, multicolored, tattoos and drawings blanket Medaelia's hands and arms. The 'Play' and 'Pause' buttons.

She winks at them with her right eye. At first, Muta's eyes gravitate toward the tattoo around her right eye, before flicking down to her hands. On the back of one of them, Paerce's trifurcated arrow, the arrowheads point at Muta, flashing between green and red.

They stand, drawing their daggers, clenching their teeth as they point at the affront to Paerce's creativity. "You probably think that perhaps, I have forgotten how this game is played."

They gesture at their professors, who gape at Paerce's plagiarized tattoo.

Medaelia's undeterred. Her lips upturn into an outline of a smile. "But allow me to remind you: This is an experiment. The faculty? Students? They willingly joined."

Muta raises an eyebrow. "I assumed the rigors of finals week—on everyone—would dampen attendance. And enthusiasm."

Medaelia draws a circle in the air with her index finger, pointed down like a compass' drawing arm. "But professors inflicted unintended casualties, nonetheless…"

Muta nods, the image of the bisected student's body rising up from where they buried it in their thoughts. "How many professors did you want to kill?"

Medaelia doesn't answer, instead turning her probing eyes to Muta's friends, shaking her head at them. Muta presses, "How many students—"

Medaelia sits up straighter and mocks slits her throat with her index finger. Students turn to her, some shaken, others firm, all without her breaking eye contact. "I would've died for them."

The crowd nods. Muta frowns but doesn't break eye contact. "Your experiment was self-defeating. Only passionate people came—not a representative sample. You didn't ask students—us—about course diversity."

Medaelia relaxes, and her eyes flick down to the tabletop.

Muta presses, "You're explaining this for you—not us. We're dead meat."

They lean in and slash their daggers in front of them, the two strikes crossing, the pommel spurs mock puncturing their own throat. "You've got me in a... chokehold."

Energy rises and falls in Medaelia's eyes, alongside the reality Muta offers, their elongated cadence. She clasps her hands in front of her.

Ellison claps her hands. Wires snake out of Medaelia's seat back, tear her hood off, shorn her blonde hair off at her shoulders, and scissor inward.

Medaelia's undeterred.

From behind Muta, Ellison screams and levitates. Two icons flare up on Medaelia's arms: The mirrored halves of a white heart, outlined in dark blue. The wires detach. She rises and crosses the room without looking back. as Ellison leverages her feet against the tabletop, but doesn't budge, Muta can neither stifle their gasp, nor muster enough shame to stop gawking. "Go," she mouths.

Dread wells up, but Muta's intrigue overpowers it. They follow Medaelia toward an ajar closet door at the back of the room. Medaelia points to Two bodies behind it, propped open by boxes in strobing light. She motions for Muta to enter first.

They obey.

A man's head, his decapitated torso, and a woman, lie on the floor, inches apart. muscle, blood vessels, and bones, yanked apart, hang in ragged strands from the decapitation points at his head and neck, contrasting with Lyle's precise, compass incisions hours earlier. Cables with frayed wires snake out of the frames of his glasses, and blue, glowing shards from the lenses riddle his face and the linoleum floor.

Accompanying the glasses, a thin screen covers his face and wraps around the front, upper half of his head, a lightweight, pragmatic VR visor. More cabling in the edges frames the visor, allowing it to change shape. Even as Muta watches, ghostly images of his face, emoji, and emoticons, race across it. The exposed lithium battery fizzles on his temple, the silver metal, resembling butter, corroding as they watch.

A smart watch adorns his right wrist, and a second flexible display gloves his hand. Through the hand screen, thinner than the one on the man's head, Muta pinches the lattice of cabling holding it together. The smashed remains of both devices' screens glow a residual blue. A dongle, used to project the data from the watch to his head mounted screen, impales his palm. Even in death, the man shields his chest with his right hand, fingers extended in a claw-like shape. Slashes to the bone shred the skin between his fingers: Self-defense wounds. A stranded name tag, separated from its lanyard, flutters on the man's—Dr. Ash's—chest. Tears prickle at the corners of Muta's eyes, splattering on their T-shirt—

The salt of someone else's tears coats their tongue and their dry cheeks. They speak in Kayleigh's voice.

"You corrupted Jim in a heartbeat, you bitch. How many seconds did it take you to kill him?"

Taking even breaths and unmoving from her relaxed posture, Medaelia waits for Muta to examine Dr. Jim Ash's body to their satisfaction. The genuine anger that possessed them subsides.

THESIS

As Muta glimpses the woman, dizziness assaults them. They clutch their temples. The woman's skull blows apart, shockwaves at the back of her head spreading from the epicenter forward and outward, the ringing of a gunshot crashing over them. Muta's hands rise to chest height, mimicking the grip on a shotgun. Their ears ache, and their stomach churns. A single drop of blood trickles from their nostril onto their lower lip.

Before they can ask how Medaelia knows about Camerin utilizing this same cause of death, the woman's body discolors. Flesh, muscle, bone, liquify, and seep into the sagging floor, confined to a rectangle outlining her. Liquid pools and disappears near her feet, like water swirling down a bathtub drain.

In the next moment, vertebral fragments and dismembered limbs surround her corpse.

Their eyes rack focus from the blood soaked floor beneath the woman's body to her torso. As they watch, her spine crumples like a soda can. They home in on her name tag, the next time it rematerializes. They can't find Freeman's cause of death.

Medaelia lets go of Muta and mimes wielding a katana, before compressing her hands together. The counterattack bursts free, Cydni's most outraged shouts clawing up and out of Muta's own throat: "Is your cause just? Or is that just what you tell yourself!?"

Medaelia is undeterred. The entire time, she holds them firm, unflinching.

Unzipping her hoodie, she reveals scabbed and fresh scars, blanketing her shoulders and neck. Her bloodstained shirt and jeans, blending into the background darkness, pop in the impossible LED light. Muta winces. "Why'd they attack you?"

The professor gestures for Muta to return to their table. Muta double taps their ravenous curiosity before they ask a question they'll regret. They catch faint whispers around them, but otherwise, students continue talking, eating, or sleeping at ease, as if the room isn't propped up with makeshift barricades, or the electricity isn't compromised. Next to the door, a pair of blank eyes in an exploded skull, HF, the chemical formula for hydrofluoric acid written in a dripping script, and a katana cocooned in motion blur lines, graffiti the wall. Each symbol comprises the center of a grid of triangles, inscribed in a circle. The glowing colors of similar drawings or diagrams invade blank space on the other walls of the cafeteria, the glowing ink substituting for the dim emergency light.

Medaelia notices them looking around and points at scavenged, metal tables, their legs rewelded to fasten them to the doorframe, to brace the entrance shut. She glares daggers at the blood that streaks the floor inches beyond the threshold. Her nostrils and facial tattoo flare, as she retakes her seat.

Ellison lowers to the ground. She pivots on her heel toward the barred doors, bloodstained threshold, and Medaelia's injuries. Her two razor thin whips clicking against each other at the air betray her anger. "How long ago did Jim and Maxine attack?"

Medaelia shrugs. "For the news? Patrick? Lex? The Discyples server?

"A week?

"For the four of you?

"A day. More or less."

Camerin, pale and shaking, leans on Davies's shoulder. Muta seizes his other wrist, fingers raking at the multicolored cables; Camerin doesn't hide his affirming nod. Rennie stabilizes his friend in a stable posture before squaring up to Medaelia. "How'd you sabotage my code—"

Medaelia doesn't respond.

"It was her experiment," Muta reasons aloud. "Her cabin, her rules."

Medaelia's lips curl into an unmistakable smile. Everyone shudders, except Ellison. She closes in on Medaelia, her resentment tightening her braided whips.

"Davies? She cut us off before we... Before we became informed participants."

Muta points at Medaelia's media playback tattoos. She nods once. Her expression remains unchanged, but she looks down for an instant.

Camerin counters, "This isn't an experiment. But she never said the staff could leave. Or clarified what we could disclose. She handcuffed us to the table."

Medaelia doesn't respond.

Muta skims the crowd. A student charges a laptop with a power bank, the barrel of a firearm—

Muta blinks. His firearm, leaning against his chair, lacks a mechanism to chamber bullets, and a chamber of any kind, instead featuring a wildly pulsating blue gem where the magazine should be. An antenna juts up from his helmet.

At the far end of the room, a woman draws on a sheet of butcher paper, the pommel of a longsword, shaped like a bear's head, inches from her elbow. The rippled, dark gray steel, contrasts against her jacket and the tiled floor.

"Why are you bribing them with gifts? Offerings? Sacrifices?"

In turn, Muta tilts their head toward each student. "Offer them a weapon to make them feel safe—so they won't leave?"

Medaelia doesn't respond.

Knuckles bleached white, Camerin props himself upright against the edge of the table. "The how and when don't matter. Only that the future doesn't belong to you"

A] appears on Davies's vambraces, completing the bottom line of code. On its own, the camera detaches from Muta, panning over and zooming in on Camerin and Ellison. Camerin twists his bracelets around his stiffened fingers, separating them from each other. Medaelia's hands grow rigid.

More glowing code scrawls onto Ellison's arm, her wires detaching and converging on Medaelia in coordinated segments. They gash the tabletop as they pass by. Ellison twitches her fingers; the wires emulate Camerin's bracelets.

Medaelia's undeterred: Wires burrowing into her flesh, she claps her hands. The interlocking, triangular tattoos on her arms flare. The spikes in her facial tattoo sharpen. The wires fragment.

Davies flips his table, shielding him from the neck down, and tackles Medaelia. He sunders the clip securing her pen to her lapel with one hand and flings the pen out of reach and toward Ellison's cupped palms with the other. He seizes Medaelia's shoulders, blocking her view with his body, and slams his shoulder into her at full force.

Muta draws their daggers, lunging toward Medaelia's eye with one, and toward her jugular artery.

Vision obscured, blood streaming down her right eyebrow, and fingers fractured, Medaelia claps again. The wires reform into a net that intercepts and redirects Muta's ambush, inches from Davies's eyes.

He and Muta put their hands up. Camerin drops his bracelets, but yelps as they rebound. Ellison sneers, as Medaelia disentangles Muta's daggers. Her belt unloops from her waist and shears a leg off of Davies's table. Her staff points toward Medaelia. She winds the wire around one end and hefts the other, in the same two handed grip that Muta taught Camerin. She spats, "Go on. Tell us how you easily outwitted us, all of us! Tell us how we made your great transcendence possible. Even though we didn't know what it was."

Muta can't help but smile. Ellison reciprocates. Her fingertips crackle, the lights flickering as she saps electricity from them and channels it into her staff. Arcs radiate from her combat Tesla coil.

Medaelia's undeterred. Her torn fingertips quiver, directing the camera at the doors, quaking on their hinges. Muta's stomach drops.

Muta grinds their heel into the linoleum. The illusion—vision?—flashes around them, of the tables

THESIS

tumbling off of the floor above, pixilating before vanishing. Medaelia, bleeding, battered, and staring down multiple causes of death, commands order into the conversation, from Muta's chaos.

Blunt force trauma hammers Muta—and everyone's—skulls.

Behold. A thesis.

'15

INTERIOR, CAFETERIA, IV

The main doors cave in. JASON and RENEE, drenched in blood, encrusted with debris, enter. JASON types data points into his hovering, chest height graphing calculator. Sharper versions of the numerical apparitions encircle MUTA and project on the inside of their eyelids. MEDAELIA claps her hands. Empty tables and loose rubble transmute into a barricade, shielding the remaining students. Behind it, they raise improvised and alchemical weapons.

JASON'S graph, above RENEE'S head, has an x-axis marked with 0 through 12, and a y-axis with only the zero minimum marked. JASON confirms each entry, and inflicts matching wounds on RENEE, by jabbing his body with his index finger. MUTA shudders. JASON'S voice overrides theirs.)

MUTA

Misguided. Rash. Incomplete. Unsubstantiated.

(RENEE flings chunks of the floor and walls at JASON with her spring. CAMERIN speaks with her voice, over the crunching of the cafeteria tearing apart.)

CAMERIN

Cold. Rigid. Detached. Unrealistic.

(Multiplying JASON'S data set alters the text's orbit. Growing or shrinking the data set size thickens or thins the text, deflecting RENEE'S attacks. RENEE gashes his forearm, within his defenses. JASON doesn't stop. CAMERIN sighs. Hands over their face, MUTA'S transfixed. MEDAELIA rounds the table. Beside them, she films the fight by hand.)

MUTA

But Jason loved Daniel—so why Renee?

(JASON palm heel strikes and stomps the air and nearby surfaces and objects to confirm data entries. Data fragments and material he touches hurtle toward Engle. MUTA gapes at the projectiles' trajectories, identical to the debris MUTA circumvented to reach CAMERIN. RENEE draws blood with her spring before *launching it a JASON. He neither dodges nor slows. His graph's x-axis creeps rightward. MUTA indicates R^2 = 0.75 above the y-axis.)*

MUTA

Who caused the other 25 percent of his blood loss?

(DAVIES'S eyes dilate and glow. All text clears from his vambraces. He grits his teeth, his trembling hands clinging to CAMERIN'S heaving shoulders.)

CAMERIN

Fuck correlation—they should be dead!

MEDAELIA

To them, death doesn't matter. I know firsthand.

(RENEE pierces JASON'S palm with her spike and dislocates his shoulder with her hook before he can finish entering his next data point. As both new wounds bleed, and blood obscures the display, the calculator wavers. MUTA frowns. He enters another series of data points, but the text drips, like wet ink down a page. RENEE'S posture straightens, and her freshest wounds close, leaving jagged scars. MUTA nods at MEDAELIA. ELLISON shakes her head multiple times.)

PAULINE UGALDE

ELLISON
Fuck no!

DAVIES
There's nothing left of them.

(CAMERIN pries DAVIES'S hands off him. He turns MUTA toward him, and his eyes go blank. He ties his wrists behind his back, chest heaving. MUTA'S breath syncs with him, their arms wrenching behind their back, daggers flinging from their now open hands. CAMERIN'S eyes lock on their winged, golden strawberry pin. The illusory, calming feather golden from the admissions office appears but tears apart. As they struggle, they mouth CAMERIN'S words. he speaks with CYDNI'S voice.)

CAMERIN and **CYDNI** (voiceover, in MUTA'S ear)
I'm just trying to help you…

(Slick with blood from wounds on RENEE'S right eyebrow and throat, the spring slingshots toward JASON'S temple. MUTA headbutts CAMERIN, their wrists popping out from behind their back as he scrabbles at his face. They backhand MEDAELIA'S jaw, elbow her nose, and seize the camera.)

THESIS

ELLISON
Not you too!

(ELLISON and DAVIES converge on MUTA, who stomps on his foot, before sliding under both professors' reach, and Yanking ELLISON off balance with one of her astray wires. Students fire kinetic and energy weapons from behind the barricade. The projectiles shatter JASON'S shield. Poised for a closeup of Engle's face, they leap in front of JASON, arms outspread. The spike punctures their cheek. The hook catches between two exterior notepads in Daniel's vest opposite from their duct tape patch, rips the splayed open notebook underneath, and stabs into their chest. Engle and JASON collapse. Artifacts clanging to the ground, their eyes dim,, as each examines their rival's injuries anew.)

MUTA
You can stop now.

(The combatants gravitate toward the impaled vest and MUTA'S blood oozing across it. Both look away, even as MUTA pans the camera over them.)

MUTA
We can heal you—

159

PAULINE UGALDE

(The combatants shake their heads, sapped of the energy to speak. JASON pinches a sheet from Daniel's vest between his fingers, his and MUTA'S blood congealing to the page. Teeth gritted, he tears it out. It's a hardcopy of one of Daniel's drawing annotations on Kill Counting: bloodied gears forming a spiral. MUTA weeps.)

MUTA

We can dull the pain—

(Gesturing for the crying MUTA to sit, both rivals cut them off. They comply. RENEE pushes the spring across the floor toward JASON. JASON telekinetically offers RENEE his calculator. They take turns reading the page from Daniel's vest, before returning it to MUTA.

Staring into the camera, JASON embeds the hook in his jugular artery, threads the spring through his neck, and plants the spike into his right eye and out the back of his skull. RENEE enters data until the points $x = 12$ and $R\char`\^2$ almost equals 1 on JASON'S graph, and mars the data set with an inclining, rightward line. With her index finger, she replicates the line and duplicates JASON'S injuries by pointing at the same sites on her body. Both artifacts disintegrate.

160

THESIS

Still bleeding, MEDAELIA strides toward MUTA, kneels, and films herself binding their wounds with her jacket. She takes Engle and Bates' photos, her and MUTA'S blood clinging to her hands. Muta's professors watch from the table and surround the pair when she's finished. The hiding students emerge from behind the barricade and form a perimeter around the group.)

'16

EXTERIOR, STEVENS CREEK BLVD, CUPERTINO, CALIFORNIA

Mute shock carries Muta out of the cafeteria and off the campus grounds.

Did they faint? Is Camerin channeling his vision into them? Did Ellison plug one of her wires into the back of their head, into the matrix?

Did Medaelia compel me to hallucinate? Did she stop?

After several minutes—or was it hours?—Muta lies on a makeshift stretcher. Medaelia tilts their cupped chin upward. They open their eyes, entering her firing line of sight. They sit up.

Sunlight streams into their dilated pupils. A sheet of sweat throttles their body. Their parched throat emits a hoarse gasp. Dizziness overtakes them, and they topple headlong.

A fine, wire net scoops them up. Their symptoms subside, a circular, gentle pressure massages their temples, without anyone touching them. Camerin trickles water into their agape mouth. Only after they've parched their thirst, does their phone float over to them. It reads five past two P.M., on June 19th: A week after they submitted their final projects and senior thesis. Medaelia takes their shoulders in her hands as They look behind them. Beyond the MacReady Building's dark parking lot, campus lights flicker in erratic patterns. Medaelia's media playback icons glow. The rewind arrow shines red, fading as illusory, purple ink shades her 'Play' button anew. Muta angles their phone, illuminating their collarbone and face. Closed, but jagged scars replace their puncture wounds. Circular scars model Medaelia's fingers, and jagged lines split her crooked nose, throat, and eyebrow. A bruise paints her chin and lower lip.

The diligent camera, still recording, floats from Ellison's hands to Muta's. They pan it over the campus and their friends, and fasten it to their shoulder.

In the distance, a figure runs toward the group. Eyes shielded, Muta sprawls backward again.

Camerin springs forward and catches them.

Facing Muta, he touches code blocks around his wrists and bracelets. Even while a cold pack adheres to his cheeks and forehead, he maintains a genuine smile. Ellison raises her sparking hands and a wire a garrote. Davies's vambraces erect floating code.

Medaelia imposes herself between Muta and the stranger, arms spread, brandishing her pen like a sword. Muta tracks the person, zooming in on a familiar winged, golden, strawberry pin then the glint of a raised pepper spray can, nozzle pointed forward. They crouch and Paerce rolls on impact, after leaping from a height. Eyes that aren't their own, and a camera attached to a form fitting body harness, zooms in on their own rig and face in kind. Daniel's rendition of Kayleigh's tattoo design superimposes over their vision in their right eye.

The group grins in unison, as Paerce recovers from his leap off a building and beckons behind him. Cydni and Kayleigh follow, recognizable via their pins and camera setups. Kayleigh hobbles on a staff, leaning on Cydni's unincumbered shoulder.

Medaelia laughs, gentle but firm. She squeezes Muta's hand and faces Paerce, as he makes a lithe, relaxed vault over a car.

Armed police, rooted in place, drop their professionalism, overt shock accompanying the crouched Paerce ascending alongside a blast proof barricade. He reorients his body in midair, in time with Cydni pressing her palms together, as if praying.

Sliding—ultra dashing—across the street, she syncs her dashes with her footfalls.

She hefts Kayleigh on her back. The professors' eyes go blank, as the stylized prayer rings out, crackling with radio static.

Even if it hurts me?

Her lips contort around the pleading, almost reverent, cadence. Limbs secured around Cydni's torso and neck, Kayleigh's bloodshot eyes widen in recognition.

Muta slams the camera onto their shoulder, clasps their hands in elation.

Show me the way.